PRAISE FOR BILL PRONZINI,
2008 MYSTERY WRITERS OF AMERICA GRAND MASTER

"One of the best in the mystery-suspense field."
—*The Washington Post Book World*

"There is no living writer whose work more faithfully embodies the spirit of classic private-eye fiction than Bill Pronzini's. [It is] classy, classy noir storytelling."   —*The Plain Dealer* (Cleveland)

"It is hard to find a better crime writer . . . Pronzini has won or been nominated for every award known to mystery fiction."
—*Library Journal*

"The Nameless Detective novels are a thinking reader's detective series."   —*Chicago Sun-Times*

"The best rock 'n' roll songs are 2 minutes 50 seconds long, and the best short detective novels are written by Bill Pronzini. In both genres you are drawn in immediately, have a lot of fun, and when it's over, you look ahead to the next time."
—*The Boston Globe*

"NAMELESS DETECTIVE" MYSTERIES BY BILL PRONZINI

Schemers
Fever
Savages
Mourners
Nightcrawlers
Scenarios (collection)
Spook
Bleeders
Crazybone
Boobytrap
Illusions
Sentinels
Spadework (collection)
Hardcase
Demons
Epitaphs
Quarry
Breakdown
Jackpot
Shackles
Deadfall
Bones
Double (with Marcia Muller)
Nightshades
Quicksilver
Casefile (collection)
Bindlestiff
Dragonfire
Scattershot
Hoodwink
Labyrinth
Twospot (with Collin Wilcox)
Blowback
Undercurrent
The Vanished
The Snatch

FEVER

A Nameless Detective Novel

Bill Pronzini

A Tom Doherty Associates Book
New York

This is a work of fiction. All of the characters, organizations, and events portrayed in this novel are either products of the author's imagination or are used fictitiously.

FEVER: A NAMELESS DETECTIVE NOVEL

A Forge Book
Published by Tom Doherty Associates, LLC
175 Fifth Avenue
New York, NY 10010

www.tor-forge.com

Forge® is a registered trademark of Tom Doherty Associates, LLC.

The Library of Congress has catalogued the hardcover edition as follows:

Pronzini, Bill.
　　Fever : a Nameless Detective novel / Bill Pronzini.—1st hardcover
edition.
　　　　　p. cm.
　　"A Tom Doherty Associates book."
　　ISBN-13: 978-0-7653-1818-3
　　ISBN-10: 0-7653-1818-0
　　1. Nameless Detective (Fictitious character)—Fiction. 2. Private
investigators—California—San Francisco—Fiction. 3. Missing persons—
Fiction. 4. Gambling—Fiction. 5. San Francisco (Calif.)—Fiction. I. Title.
PS3566.R67F48　2008
813'.54—dc22

　　　　　　　　　　　　　　　　　　　　　　　　　　　　2008005228

ISBN-13: 978-0-7653-2290-6 (tpb.)
ISBN-10: 0-7653-2290-0 (tpb.)

First Hardcover Edition: June 2008
First Trade Paperback Edition: August 2009

Printed in the United States of America

0　9　8　7　6　5　4　3　2　1

For Judi and Fender Tucker,
ramble on!

AUTHOR'S NOTE

This novel was conceived prior to the abrupt passage of a 2006 federal law that severely restricts and criminalizes the funding of Internet gambling. The reader, therefore, should keep in mind that the events depicted herein took place before the enactment of that law, when online bettors were permitted to wager as much and as often as they liked, and could finance their bets with credit cards, electronic fund transfers, and personal checks.

FEVER

1

It took us a week to find Janice Krochek. The little piece of irony in that was, the entire time she was living in an apartment hotel less than fifteen blocks from our South Park offices.

Not that we could have had any idea of her whereabouts at the start, aside from the fact that her husband believed she was somewhere in San Francisco. It was the fourth time in four years that she'd disappeared from their Oakland Hills home. The other times, the city was where she'd gone; the longest she'd stayed away was six days, and she'd always returned home voluntarily. This time, she'd been missing twelve days before Mitchell Krochek filed a missing person report, and three weeks before he decided to hire private investigators. It wasn't that he was unconcerned, he said; it was just that he'd been through it all so many times and his financial situation was shaky, thanks to his wife and her compulsion.

Jake Runyon was the one who finally located her.

Bloodhound Jake. In the days when I ran a one-man agency I was a pretty good field man; tenacious, the way you have to be in order to pay the bills. Runyon was something else again. His instincts were sharper, his tenacity greater, than those of any investigator I'd ever known, public or private.

I was in the office when he called in. Early afternoon on a slow November Tuesday, Tamara and I and our new hire, Alex Chavez, all doing routine work. Janice Krochek was at the Hillman, on Leavenworth just off Jones, staying with a waitress named Ginger Benn who'd been picked up once on a prostitution rap—the call-girl variety. Working as a call girl herself, possibly, although Runyon couldn't verify it. She was in the apartment now, he said. Did I want him to brace her?

I thought about it. "No," I said, "Tamara and I will handle it. You've got other work to move on. Where are you now?"

"Hillman's lobby."

"We'll be there in fifteen minutes."

Tamara had been listening through the open connecting door between our offices. When I hung up, she said, "You and Tamara will do what?"

"Go talk to Janice Krochek. Jake just found her."

"Where?"

I repeated what Runyon had told me.

"Call girl? Terrific. Her husband'll be real pleased."

"He doesn't necessarily have to know that part of it. Depends on what she says and what she decides to do."

Tamara sighed. "Both of us, huh?"

"Unless you want to talk to her alone."

"No way! I was thinking maybe you don't need me . . ."

"Better if there's another woman present. Easier on everybody."

"Says you."

"Says the voice of experience."

The thing about a case like this one, where an adult subject has disappeared voluntarily, is that a private investigative agency is ethically obligated to consult with the subject before reporting his or her whereabouts to the client. Did Janice Krochek want her husband to know where she was, want him to come to her, want us to take her to him? The decision was entirely hers. If we reported to the husband first, without consulting with her, we'd be wide open to a harassment lawsuit. I'd informed Mitchell Krochek of this before we accepted the case. It hadn't changed his mind; his main interest right now, he said, was in knowing that she was safe. So we'd written a clause into the agency contract, and he'd signed it, and now here we were at crunch time. I was not looking forward to it any more than Tamara was.

The Hillman was on the edge of the Tenderloin, a few blocks from downtown—a tweener neighborhood inhabited by a polyglot of small businesses, Vietnamese, Cambodian, and other Asian families, transients, welfare recipients, drug dealers, hookers. Venerable stone pile, four stories, caramel-colored, with a banner strung above the narrow entrance that proclaimed UNDER NEW MANAGEMENT in faded red letters. Once, a long time ago, it had been a regular hotel catering to tourists on a budget; the transformation into apartment hotel had been gradual and was probably now complete. The kind of place you wouldn't want to live in if you had other options, even if you were only sharing space with somebody else.

The lobby was cut up into a pair of small rooms connected by an archway, one of them containing the desk and a few pieces of musty furniture haphazardly arranged, the other a common room dominated by a big TV set whose now-blind eye peered out at you as you walked in.

"Nice place," Tamara said, wrinkling her nose. "If you like the smell of Lysol."

"Big comedown for a woman like Janice Krochek." The home she shared with her husband in the Oakland Hills was a million bucks' worth of real estate.

"People and their screwed-up lives."

"That's the main reason we're in business, kiddo."

"Don't I know it."

Runyon had been sitting on one of the chairs opposite the desk. Not doing anything else, just sitting there with his legs together and his hands flat on his knees. Patience was one of his long suits. That, and the ability to shut himself down when he was waiting, like a piece of finely tuned machinery with an idle switch. Part of the reason was his training as a cop: he'd been on the Seattle PD for years before a leg injury pensioned him off and led him into private investigative work. The other part of the reason was the loss of his wife to ovarian cancer a couple of years ago, after twenty years of marriage. He was still grieving—from all indications, he might never stop.

He got slowly to his feet when he saw us, stood flat-footed

with no expression on his big, slablike face. Habitual, that lack of expression. He seldom displayed emotion of any kind; the one I'd never seen was joy.

The three of us formed a circle. The desk clerk, a youngish guy with thinning, rust-colored hair, was watching us, and I wondered briefly what he was thinking. One sixty-plus craggy Italian male, one forty-something stoic WASP male, one twenty-six-year-old black woman—three generations, three individuals completely different from one another.

"Still in her room, Jake?" I asked.

"Unless she went down the fire escape. She had a visitor, just after I called."

"A john?"

"Not unless he's a rabbit. He was out in less than ten minutes."

"How do you know he saw her?"

"Heard him ask the clerk for Ginger Benn's room. She's out—it was Krochek he wanted. Thirties, heavyset, expensive clothes."

"Pimp?"

"I don't think so," Runyon said. "I followed him outside when he left. He had a car waiting."

"You get the license plate?"

"I got it. Car's a white Caddy, looked brand new."

Tamara said, "I'll check it out when we get back," and he gave her the page from his notebook with the number written on it.

I asked, "Krochek using her own name?"

"Maiden name. Janice Stanley."

"Apartment number?"

"Three-oh-nine. Third floor."

"Okay. We'll take it from here, Jake."

He nodded and moved off to the front door. On the way to the elevators, I called over to the desk man, "We're going up to see the woman in three-oh-nine. Don't bother to announce us."

That bought me a faint sneer and a mock salute. "Yes sir, officer, whatever you say."

I didn't tell him we weren't cops; let him think what he wanted. We got into one of a pair of elevators and it clanked and jolted us up to three. The car smelled of disinfectant, same as the lobby; so did the upstairs hallway. 309 was off an ell toward the rear. I rattled my knuckles on the panel.

Pretty soon a woman's voice said warily, "Who is it?"

"Mrs. Krochek, Janice Krocheck?"

There was a silence. Then, "That you again, Mr. Lassiter?"

"No. Open up, please."

More silence. Then a chain rattled and a deadbolt clicked and the door edged open about three inches. The eye that peered out was brown and faintly bloodshot. It roamed narrowly over me, over Tamara. "Who are you? I don't know you."

"We're here on behalf of your husband."

"Oh, shit." More annoyed than anything else. "Police?"

"Private investigators."

"You're kidding."

We flashed our licenses.

"Mitch must be desperate," she said. "Is he out there with you?"

"No. Mind if we talk inside?"

She said, "Of course I mind," but the protest had no teeth in it; the chain rattled again, and I heard it drop down against the inside panel. When I pushed on the door, it opened inward and she was walking away across the room in quick, jerky strides. Tamara and I went in and I shut the door.

Two-room apartment, bedroom and sitting room. Not large, not tidy, the furniture old and scratched up, the carpet threadbare. The dominant smell in there was tobacco smoke, thick and acrid; my chest tightened almost at once. Janice Krochek sat down on an open, unmade sofa bed and reached for a package of Newports on an end table.

I said, "I'd appreciate it if you didn't smoke."

She said, "I live here, you don't," and put one of the cancer sticks in her mouth and fired it with a cheap lighter. "How'd you find me?"

"It wasn't too hard," Tamara said.

"You don't look like detectives. Either of you."

"You don't look like what you are, either."

I gave Tamara a warning look. She's young and she can be less than tactful; she needs to work on her people skills. We'd decided that she should do most of the talking, woman to woman, but if necessary I'd have to take over. There was nothing to be gained in allowing the situation to turn adversarial.

Janice Krochek laughed—an empty, sardonic sound. She was not at ease sitting there. High-strung type, but it was more than that—a sense of nervous expectancy, not for what we had to say to her but for something else. As late as it was, she might have just gotten out of bed. She wore a loose man's shirt over a pair of jeans, her feet were bare, and her short brown hair was uncombed. She was thirty-three, but in the dim light, and without makeup, she looked older; you could see the stress lines around her mouth and eyes. Addiction will do that to you, no matter what type of addiction it happens to be.

She said, "Why did Mitch hire you? He couldn't possibly want me back after all this time."

Tamara said, "He could and he does."

"Well, then, he's a damn fool."

"Lots of damn fools running around these days."

That didn't bother her, either. "I suppose he told you all about me."

"He told us enough."

"All about my 'sickness.' That's what he calls it."

"What do you call it?"

"The sweetest high there is," she said. It was not a natural or spontaneous response, but the kind of phrase a person hears somewhere and likes enough to appropriate and repeat as their own. "He wants it cured. I don't."

"Even though you keep losing, getting in deeper and deeper."

"I don't care about that. The money isn't important, winning or losing. Either of you ever gamble for high stakes? Poker, craps, whatever?"

"No."

"Then you can't understand any more than Mitch does. The action, the excitement . . . there's nothing else like it. I'd rather gamble than fuck."

That last was intended to shock, but neither of us re-
acted. Tamara said, "One supports the other now, right?"

"What's that supposed to mean?"

"We know what you've been doing for money since you
left home."

I nudged Tamara this time, from where Janice Krochek
couldn't see me doing it. Krochek started to say something—
and there was a sudden melodic jangling from across the
room, the kind of programmed tune fragment that substi-
tutes for ringing in modern cell phones. She came off the
sofa and went after it blur-fast, like a cat uncoiling to chase a
mouse. The brown eyes were avid—the first real animation
she'd shown. Before the phone rang again she had it out of
her handbag and flipped open. She said, "Yes?" and then listened with her body turned away from us.

The conversation didn't last long. I heard her say,
"That's too bad, I was hoping . . . okay, if that's the way it
has to be. Later, then? Right." She dropped the phone back
into the bag, and when she turned, the avidity and animation were gone. She recrossed the room in the same jerky
strides as when she'd let us in.

She didn't sit down again. Bent for another Newport,
blew a thick stream of smoke, and said through it, "Well?
What happens now?"

"That's up to you, Mrs. Krochek," Tamara said.

"Stanley, Ms. Janice Stanley. I like that name better."

"You're still married to the man."

"You can't force me to go back to him."

"That's right, we can't."

"Already tell him where to find me?"

"No. You want us to?"

"Christ, no. It's all over between us. I made that clear to him before I left."

"Man's willing to pay all your outstanding debts if you give the marriage one more try."

"Sure he is, so I won't divorce him. That's the real reason he hired you. Lot cheaper for him to pay off my debts than give me half of everything he's got."

"Everything he's got left," Tamara said pointedly.

"It was mine as much as his, then and now. You think he's some kind of saint?" Bitter and angry now. "Well, he's not. Far from it. He's looking out for number one, same as I am."

"You don't believe he wants what's best for you?"

"I don't care if he does or doesn't. I like to gamble. And I like my freedom."

"How about selling your body? You like that, too?"

If there was any shame left in the woman, she had it well hidden behind the wall of her compulsion. She said flatly, "I don't know what you're talking about."

"Real hard way to support yourself and that habit of yours."

"What I do for money until the divorce is my business."

"Not when it's against the law."

"So what're you saying? You're going to report me to the police? You can't prove I've been hooking and neither can they."

"Not unless they catch you at it."

Time for me to step in, try a different tack. I said, "Have you seen a lawyer, Mrs. Krochek?"

"Lawyer? About the divorce? No, not yet."

"Why not, if you're so dead set on it?"

"That's my business."

"It doesn't cost that much to hire one."

"Never mind about that. If Mitch doesn't file, I will—soon. You tell him that."

"How much do you owe Lassiter?"

She didn't like that question; it made her even more edgy. She took a quick drag on her cigarette before she said, "Who?"

"The man who came to see you a little while ago."

"How do you know about that? Spying on me?"

"It's a reasonable question."

"I don't owe him anything."

"Whoever he works for then. Loan shark?"

"That's none of your damn business."

"The same shark you borrowed from before? The one who threatened you?"

A muscle jumped in her cheek. "Mitch's fantasy. He listened in on a phone call and misinterpreted what he heard, that's all."

"That's not what he says."

"Well, I'm telling you the way it was."

"So no threats then and none now. No pressure."

"That's right. No heat at all."

"Okay. Your business, your life."

"Now you're getting it. You going to tell Mitch where I'm living or not?"

"Not without your consent."

"I figured as much. Suppose he tries to pry it out of you? Offers to pay you extra?"

"We don't operate that way."

"So what are you going to tell him?"

"We found you, you seem to be in reasonably good health, you say you're not in any danger, you don't want to reconcile, and you're going to file for divorce any day."

"And to leave me the hell alone from now on."

"If that's what you want."

"Exactly what I want. So go tell him."

I laid a business card, the one with both my name and Tamara's on it, on the stained top of a cabinet. "In case you have second thoughts or want to talk some more."

"I won't. Now get out."

Gladly, I thought. The damn smoke in there was bothering my lungs, making my throat feel scratchy. As soon as Tamara and I were out the door, Krochek came over and put the deadbolt and the chain back on. Locking herself away in her carcinogenic cocoon, to nurse her fever and wait for the phone to ring again.

In the elevator Tamara said, "Well, that was fun."

"Yeah. Pretty much what I expected."

"You know what I wanted to do in there? Bitch-slap that woman upside the head."

"Wouldn't have done any good. Hitting somebody with her kind of sickness never does."

"Guess not. I didn't do such a good job on the woman-to-woman thing, did I."

"No, but I didn't do much better."

"You think she really believes all that stuff she said? About the sweetest high and not wanting to be cured?"

"Convinced herself it's what she wants. She's a textbook case."

"She was lying about nobody threatening her."

"Lying or pretending. She didn't seem scared."

"Riding for a big fall, you ask me. Straight down the toilet."

"It's her life," I said. "She's the only one who can save it."

2

You hear a lot these days about drug addiction and alcohol addiction, but not so much about the equally widespread and growing problem of compulsive gambling. I'd come into contact with it peripherally over the years—when you've been an investigator as long as I have, you brush up against just about every kind of addiction, felony, misdemeanor, social issue, and human being there is—but I hadn't confronted it head on until Mitchell Krochek walked into the agency offices eight days ago. What he'd told me, and what Tamara had found out on an Internet search, amounted to a real eye-opener.

Gambling is a national pastime and a national mania. Las Vegas, Reno, the entire state of Nevada. Nearly two hundred and fifty Native American casinos on tribal lands in twenty-two states and more being built every year. Upwards of eighty riverboat and dockside casinos in six states. Horse tracks, dog tracks. Twenty-four-hour card rooms and private poker clubs. The Super Bowl and the World

Series and the NCAA basketball tournament and fantasy sports leagues and any number of other sporting events that fatten the bank accounts of legal sports books and illegal bookie operations in every city of any size in the country. State lotteries. Dozens of online sites devoted to poker and other games of chance designed to separate bettors from their hard-earned money. Even those old standbys, slot machines, were making a comeback thanks to the budget woes of local governments.

All but two states in the union have some form of legalized gambling, with an estimated annual take for the industry of $75 billion. California alone approaches $15 billion in annual gambling revenue, owing in large part to the sixty Native American casinos currently operating in the state, with more to come.

That's a lot of lure and a lot of money. Most people who succumb to one form of gambling or another are casual bettors—people like me, who play poker now and then, who buy lottery tickets or spend a few days a year making the rounds of the Vegas glitz palaces. Then there are the professionals, the high rollers, who earn a living from tournaments or private games and who have learned when to ride a streak and when to quit. And then there are the addicts like Janice Krochek. Men and women who don't have the skill to consistently beat the odds, who can't quit when they're losing, whose constant need for the thrill of the bet is as addictive as any drug. The estimated number of them is staggering—as many as ten million adults in the U.S. alone, according to the National Council on Problem Gambling. Combined, adult pathological gamblers and problem gamblers cost California nearly a billion dollars annually.

Most start out in small ways: lottery tickets, poker games, a day trip to one of the tracks, a weekend getaway to some casino that features electronic slots and bingo games. A few dollars here, a few dollars there, and enough wins to whet their appetites for more. That was how it had been for Janice Krochek.

She hadn't had the fever when she married Mitchell Krochek eight years ago. Hadn't had any interest in or experience with gambling at all. He'd been the gambler then, in a mild and controlled way. He liked to play blackjack and the horses once in a while; he'd introduced her to the bright lights of the Las Vegas strip, the weekend races at Bay Meadows, and the county fair circuit. Just occasional innocent fun for both of them. Until she got hooked.

Most compulsive gamblers have high underlying levels of negative emotionality: nervousness, anger, impulsiveness, feelings of being misunderstood and victimized, lack of self-discipline. Janice Krochek had all of those traits, plus what doctors call an intense dopamine cycle and an uncontrollable desire to experience the thrill that high-stakes betting provides. The psychological term is "chasing the high." Same principle, in effect, as a nymphomaniac chasing orgasm.

It was a while before Krochek realized how bad her gambling mania was. He had a fairly high-paying job as a consulting engineer and had invested in an aggressive portfolio of stocks and bonds, and he didn't keep a careful check on account balances or expenditures; she had a full complement of credit cards and did most of the bill-paying. Easy enough in the beginning for her to indulge her growing compulsion. Horses were her initial passion. She made regular visits to Bay Meadows, where she'd pore over the *Racing Form* and bet heavily on every race there as well as races at Hollywood Park and other tracks—all made easy by electronic touch screens, banks of TV screens in the trackside bar, and ATMs to supply her with more cash since she wasn't much good at picking winners or playing odds. But it didn't matter to her how often or how much she lost; the action was everything.

But Internet gambling was what really hooked her. Stud poker, Texas Hold 'Em, you name it, and all done quickly and quietly from the privacy of her own home. Instant gratification. And a pervasive trap of steady losses and increasing outlay to try to recoup. It didn't take long for the trap to close tight around her; inside of a year she dropped nearly fifty thousand dollars. That was when her husband noticed and confronted her.

She didn't try to hide it. Apologized and made the usual empty promises about quitting, seeing a therapist that specialized in neurobiologic addictions, joining Gamblers Anonymous. Instead she kept on betting larger and larger sums—and kept right on losing.

For a time she grew more clever about covering up the drain on their finances, but Krochek found out anyway and there was a big blowup. That was the first time she walked out on him. When she came back, he cut off her access to their various accounts. All that did was make her more devious. She began to pawn or sell jewelry and other possessions, to steal money out of his wallet. The cashing-in of one of their insurance policies led to another blowup, another walkout. More apologies, more empty promises. Forged checks this time, the probable secret borrowing from a loan shark, the phone call that Krochek swore was threatening. The final blowup, the final walkout. To finance this one, she'd sold her Lexus at a price well below Blue Book and everything in their house that was small enough and valuable enough to turn into quick cash.

Her total losses over four years, as near as Krochek was able to estimate: more than $200,000.

But for all of that, he claimed still to love her and to want to give her another chance. His prerogative, his money; we don't have to agree with a client's motives to take on a job. He knew going in that it was likely to be futile. Just find her, make sure she was all right, talk to her.

I felt sorry for him. Sorry for her, too; she was sick and sick people deserve pity, not censure. And sorry for myself because now I had to go tell him that there was no more hope for their marriage and not much hope for her.

Tamara had it right: people and their screwed-up lives.

Mitchell Krochek's company, Five States Engineering, had its offices on Jack London Square in Oakland. I put in a call to him as soon as Tamara and I got back to the agency offices. He was in, but about to go into a meeting and not inclined to discuss his wife's situation over the phone. Could we get together sometime after five o'clock? I said we could, and given the circumstances of what I had to tell him, I offered to drive over there rather than have him come to the city. We settled on 5:30 at the bar of a restaurant called the Ladderback.

While I was talking to him, Tamara ran a check on the license plate number Jake Runyon had given her. Technically, private investigative agencies are no longer permitted access to Department of Motor Vehicles records; a high-profile Hollywood murder case several years ago had led to a new law that kept them sealed to all but city, state, and federal law enforcement agencies. But there are ways around any law, and if you use them sparingly and judiciously, we had no qualms about it. Ethical compromise. You do what you have to in order to work a case, but you don't abuse your position of trust to clients or the public at large. The agency had a strict rule that all information gleaned through quasi-legal corner-cutting methods was kept confidential.

Tamara had established a DMV pipeline; she already had the information by the time I finished talking to Krochek. The plate number and the new Cadillac belonged to Carl M. Lassiter, with a San Francisco addresss—Russian Hill, no less. Tamara ran a cursory check on Lassiter without turning up anything. No personal history, no employment record. She asked another contact, a friend of hers, Felicia, who worked in SFPD's computer department, for a quick file search on Lassiter's name. No criminal record, no outstanding warrants of any kind. Mystery man.

That was as far as she took it. We could probably find out who Lassiter was with a deep background check, or through other sources if he was a bookie or loan shark or worked for one or the other, but there was no need unless the client specifically requested the information. We'd found Janice Krochek, we'd talked to her, and she didn't want to go home again—the job we'd been hired to do was finished. It was her business how badly she was jammed up with loan sharks or gambling interests. If Mitchell Krochek felt otherwise and wanted to try to contact Lassiter or Lassiter's employer, even without her consent, that was up to him. But if he asked me, I'd try to discourage him. In the long run it was a dead end proposition. Just like his marriage. Just like his wife's fever.

Krochek was already waiting in the crowded Ladderback bar when I walked in. I'd left the city early, because of the heavy eastbound commute traffic on the Bay Bridge, but it hadn't been too bad tonight; it was only 5:15 when I got to Jack London Square, fifteen minutes ahead of meeting time. He'd been there for a while, too, judging from the fact that he'd gotten a table and from the array of glassware in front of him—two bottles of Beck's and two shot glasses, one empty, one half-full.

His greeting was solemn; so was his handshake. Handsome guy, Krochek—blond, tanned, the tennis-and-handball type, but he didn't look so fit tonight. His lean, ascetic face was sorrowful, shadowed under the eyes, etched with stress lines. Working too hard, worrying too much.

He said, "So you found her. And the news isn't good," repeating what I'd told him on the phone. "She doesn't want me to know where she's living."

"No, she doesn't."

"Refuses to see me, try to work things out."

"No reconciliation, she said."

"Adamant about that, I suppose."

"I'm afraid so."

"She use the D word?"

"Divorce? Yes. Seems to be what she wants."

"Has she seen a lawyer?"

"Apparently not yet."

"But she's going to."

"Yes. Soon, she said."

"Throwing all her money down the gambling rathole, that's why she hasn't found herself some sleazebag already," Krochek said. "She's already blown what she got from selling her car by now, sure as hell."

"She didn't say anything about that."

"What's she doing for cash until she can squeeze more out of me? Or can't you tell me that, either?"

"Unverified, so I'd rather not say."

A waitress stopped by the table. I ordered a bottle of Sierra Nevada. Krochek said, "Another Beck's, skip the whiskey this time." That was good; at least he wasn't going to sit here and get maudlin drunk and make things even more difficult for both of us.

When the waitress went away I said, "You haven't asked how your wife is."

"All right, how is she?"

"Healthy enough. Holding herself together."

"Tense, angry, fidgety?"

"Pretty much."

"Drinking?"

"Not in front of us."

"Sure she is. Means she's betting and losing heavily. Janice doesn't touch a drop until she starts losing."

"I think she may be in debt to a loan shark."

"Wouldn't surprise me." He frowned. "You mean she's being threatened again?"

"She says no, but there's a good chance of it."

"Christ, she's stupid! You have any idea who he is?"

"Not exactly. The name Carl Lassiter mean anything to you?"

"Lassiter, Lassiter . . . no. Who's he?"

"We're not sure. Could be a shark or an enforcer for one."

"Terrific. Enforcer. A legbreaker, you mean."

"Not necessarily. Collection by coercion works just as well."

"Can you find out who he works for?"

"Probably. But if you're thinking of making direct contact to arrange to pay off her debts . . ."

"I'm not. Not anymore. It wouldn't stop her from divorcing me, now that her mind's made up. I don't want a divorce. I can't afford it."

Our drinks arrived. I had a little of my ale; he sat there staring into his half-full shot glass.

"Have you seen a lawyer, Mr. Krochek?"

"Yes, of course. He tells me there's nothing I can do, legally, if she files. Goddamn no fault, community property laws."

I didn't say anything.

"She'll get half of everything. What's left in the brokerage and savings accounts. Half of what the house and property are worth. I love that house, I worked my ass off to buy it and furnish it." He tossed the whiskey down, grimaced, and slugged a chaser from one of the Beck's bottles. "Why the hell did I ever marry her?" he said, more to himself than to me.

All of this was a different tune than the one he'd sung in my office. Then it had been the worried husband wanting his damaged wife back so he could protect her and help her deal with her addiction. Now it was the woe-is-me, she's-going-to-take-me-for-half-of-everything lament. Janice Krochek had said he was no saint, that he was motivated by self-interest; she knew him, all right. Not that you could blame him, really, after all the financial losses he'd already suffered, but still it lowered him a notch or two in my estimation.

"You'd think the divorce courts would take something like a gambling sickness into considersation," he said. "All the crap she's pulled, all the money she's blown already. But my attorney says no. The law says no fault, community property, that's it. No extenuating circumstances. She gets half of whatever I can't hide from the shyster she'll hire, and I get screwed."

Down another notch. Maybe you couldn't blame him for hiding assets, either, but it's illegal, and his telling me about it, making me an unwitting possessor of guilty knowledge, didn't set well.

"Is that fair?" he said bitterly. "After all she put me through?"

"Life can be unfair, Mr. Krochek."

"I don't need platitudes," he said. "I need a way out. Or

at least an edge of some kind. I don't suppose there's any way I can convince you to tell me where she's staying?"

"I'm sorry, no."

"I'd pay well for the information."

I let that pass. He was starting to piss me off.

"Isn't there anything more you can do?"

"Such as what?"

"I don't know," he said, "talk to her again, try to arrange a meeting so we can work something out before the lawyers get into it."

"I could make the effort, but it would be a waste of your money. I doubt she'd agree to another discussion, and even if she did, there's nothing I could say that would change her mind. It's made up, she made that plain."

"Bitch," he said. Then he said, "All right, can't you get something on her, something I can use in court? She's running around with lowlives, she could be mixed up in something illegal, couldn't she?"

"I don't think so," I said.

"You don't think she's mixed up in anything we could use?"

"I meant that it's not an investigative course we'd care to pursue."

"Why the hell not? You're a detective, aren't you?"

"With a selective list of services. Digging up dirt for use in divorce cases isn't one of them."

"So don't dig it up. Couldn't you just happen to stumble onto something somewhere? You know the kind of thing it would take—"

I was already on my feet. "End of conversation, Mr. Krochek. And end of our working arrangement."

"Wait a minute. I'm sorry, I didn't mean . . . Look, I'm desperate here, you can see that. Grabbing at straws."

"I understand and I sympathize, up to a point. You just passed that point. Good luck."

"For God's sake . . ."

I said, "You'll get our final report in the mail," and put my back to him and walked out.

3

JAKE RUNYON

He had a heavy caseload that week. The Krochek skip-trace, an employee background check for Benefield Industries, a suspicious wrongful death claim for Western Maritime and Life, and a domestic case that Tamara had taken on pro bono. That was the way he preferred it—the fuller the plate, the better. Weeks like this one, he could put in a fair amount of overtime as well as a full workday. He seldom asked for overtime pay, or even mentioned the extra hours; meals, gas and oil, and parking fees went onto the various expense accounts, that was all. Money wasn't the reason he worked long and hard. It was the activity, the need for movement and business details to occupy his time and his mind. Downtime meant the cold, empty apartment on Ortega Street and old movies on TV that did little to keep him from thinking about Colleen and the two decades they'd had together, or feeling the bitter frustration of his estrangement from Joshua.

His life wouldn't be quite so bad now if Joshua would understand that his mother's poisonous vilification had been a product of alcoholism and revenge and had no basis in fact; unbend a little, make room for some forgiveness. But that wasn't going to happen. For a time, while Runyon was investigating the gay-bashing of Joshua's unfaithful lover, he'd thought that there was a chance of establishing cordial relations, if not a reconciliation, but Andrea's brain-washing had been too complete. No contact in months now, his few phone calls unanswered; the one time he'd gone to Joshua's apartment, the partner had refused to let him in. Hopeless. If it weren't for the job, the support he'd gotten from Bill and Tamara, his move down here from Seattle would've been a total waste.

By Friday, when Tamara handed him the pro bono case, he had the rest of the load well in hand. A one o'clock in-terview in Hayward to finish up the employee background check was all for the afternoon; he said he'd be back in the city no later than four. So Tamara set up an appointment for him to meet with the new client, Rose Youngblood, at five at her home in Visitacion Valley.

It was a worried mother job: son or daughter gets into a hassle that can't or won't be taken to the police, so mom goes the private route. The agency seldom handled that kind unless the client was well-heeled, and then with reluc-tance, but recently they'd started taking on selected cases involving African-Americans, Latinos, and other minorities who needed investigative services but couldn't afford them.

Tamara's idea. Give a little something back to the community, now that the agency was solidly in the black. It was all right with Runyon. Clients were clients, corporate or individual, rich or poor.

Rose Youngblood was a black woman in her fifties, widowed and living alone in the home she'd bought with her husband thirty years ago. Employed in the admissions office at City College of San Francisco. Active in community service and church work. She hadn't contacted the agency directly; she'd been referred by Tamara's sister, Claudia, a lawyer who did some pro bono work of her own in the African-American community.

The problem was Rose Youngblood's twenty-six-year-old son, Brian. Whatever trouble he was in evidently wasn't the usual sort the twenty-something set got into these days. Stable young man with a well-paying job as a freelance computer consultant, she'd told Tamara; never gave her a moment's worry until now. Raised as a God-fearing Christian, good head on his shoulders, worked hard, had a bright future—all the proud maternal platitudes. Except that recently somebody had assaulted him, for a reason he refused to talk about, and she was fearful that his life was in jeopardy.

That was as much as Runyon knew when he parked in front of her small, wood-and-stucco home near the Crocker-Amazon Playground. One of the city's older residential neighborhoods—lower income, single-family homes, primarily owned by blacks now. On the fringe of the crime-ridden projects and driven downscale by the infestation of drugs and gangs. Drive-by shootings, burglaries, and muggings were common enough to force many residents to put up fences and security gates and bars on their windows. Rose Youngblood wasn't one of them. Living in a high-crime area, but not living in fear.

He was right on time, and she'd been watching for him; she opened the door even before he rang the bell. Tall, thin woman with gray in her close-cropped hair and stern features that conveyed determination and a strong will. Unsmiling and a little stiff at first. The first thing she said to him after he identified himself was, "Don't take this wrong, but I was hoping for a black investigator."

"We don't have one on staff for field work," Runyon said. "But the agency does have a pretty good racial mix—black, white, Latino, and Italian. I'm the token WASP."

She almost smiled. "I didn't mean to be insensitive. It's just that I don't have any idea of what's going on with my son. You understand?"

"You don't have to worry about my being able to handle it if it's racially sensitive. I was a police officer in Seattle for several years and my partner and best friend for most of them was a black man."

"I see." She opened the door for him. "Come in. It's cold out there."

Warm inside. Electric fire burning in a small living room packed with old, comfortable furniture. Two walls adorned with framed religious pictures and a brass sculpture of two hands clutching a cross. Books filled an old glass-fronted bookcase on another wall. Rose Youngblood told him to sit where he liked, took a covered rocking chair for herself, and got straight to business. No unnecessary amenities, no nonsense.

No unnecessary or repetitive information, either; she assumed what she'd told Tamara had been passed on to him and began by providing details. She wouldn't have known anything was wrong with Brian, she said, if she hadn't stopped by his flat unannounced a few days ago, after work. She hadn't heard from him in more than two weeks, which was unusual, and she'd wanted to make sure he was all right. A friend of his, Aaron Myers, had answered the door and told her Brian was ill and tried to keep her out. She'd gone in anyway and found her son on the couch, naked to the waist, his ribs taped—one of them had been cracked—and bruises all over his sides and lower back.

"Whoever beat him up must've hit him a dozen times," she said. "He couldn't control his bladder for two days afterward."

"But he wouldn't tell you who did it."

"Mugged, he said, but it wasn't the truth. I can always tell when Brian is lying. But he wouldn't budge from that story. Just said I shouldn't worry, it wouldn't happen again."

"You didn't believe him about that, either?"

"No. He sounded scared, not like himself at all. I know my son, Mr. Runyon. He's not a fearful person. It would take something bad, very bad, to put him in such a state."

She might've exaggerated the violence and Brian's state of mind; Runyon had known it to happen to other parents, even ones who claimed to "know" their kids. Nobody knew anybody, when you got right down to it. Not even themselves most of the time. Still, she wasn't the panicky, emotional type. Levelheaded. If she was concerned enough to want an investigation, there was probable cause.

He said, "Before that day, how was your son? His usual self?"

"No. Not the last few times I saw him."

"How was he different?"

"Worried about something. Upset and secretive."

"So whatever his trouble is, it's been going on for some time."

"More than a month now."

"Could it have something to do with his work?"

"I don't see how it could. He's been in computer work for five years and he's very good at it, never had any problems with the people he works for."

"Something to do with a woman?"

She frowned at the question, ran blunt fingers through her skullcap hair. "I don't see how that can be, either."

"Brian's not married, is that right?"

"He was engaged to a girl named Ginny Lawson last year, but she broke it off a month before the wedding."

"For what reason?"

"Cold feet, Brian said. The commitment and all. But it seemed sudden and out of character to me."

"As if she'd found someone else?"

"Possibly. I don't know."

"How did your son handle the breakup?"

"Not well at first. He really loved that girl."

"Angry?"

"Hurt, mostly."

"Brood about it?"

"No. He's not a man to fret over lost causes."

"Is he seeing anyone now?"

"Not that I know about."

"Tell me about his activities, what he does for recreation."

"Computers. They've been his passion ever since he was thirteen." Pride in the words. "When he's not working, he spends most of his time on the Internet."

"Chat rooms, that kind of thing?"

"I don't think so. No. He plays chess, computer chess."

"How about clubs, sports?"

"Just church activities. He met Ginny Lawson at a church dance."

Runyon said gently, "Vices, Mrs. Youngblood?"

Long, stern look. Then she said, "I suppose you have to ask that. The answer is no."

"Never any problems with liquor or drugs?"

"Never. I'd know if he'd ever been into anything like that."

Sure you would. "This friend you mentioned, Aaron Myers. Did you ask him about the beating? Away from Brian, I mean."

"Yes. He said he doesn't know what happened."

"Telling the truth or covering up?"

"I'm not sure."

"Are he and Brian close friends?"

"I don't know how close they are. They haven't known each other long, I'm pretty sure of that."

"What is it they have in common? Computers?"

"Yes."

"What does Aaron do for a living?"

"He works for a frozen food distributor, but I'm not sure which one."

"Can you tell me where he lives?"

"Somewhere near Brian. I don't have the address."

"What's your opinion of him?"

"Polite, friendly—a decent young man."

"Is there anyone else Brian is close to? Anyone who might have an idea of what led to the beating?"

She thought about it. "Well, there's Dré Janssen. They went to school together. He's one of Brian's chess opponents."

Runyon asked a few more questions, wrote down a few details in his notebook. Brian's home address and phone number. The name and address of the video store that Dré Janssen managed in the Marina. The facts that Ginny Lawson lived in San Rafael and was employed at a Wells Fargo branch in Sausalito. That was enough to start on.

"When will you start your investigation, Mr. Runyon?"

Low-priority case; he'd have to sandwich it in during the week. No purpose in telling her that. Five-thirty now, too late to do much today, but he had the weekend to fill. If he got lucky, he might get it done quick. He said, "Tomorrow, probably."

She seemed surprised. "You work Saturdays?"

"Sometimes."

"What will you do first? Talk to Brian?"

"I'm not sure yet. If I do talk to him, agency policy is not to reveal our clients' names."

"That's all right. He'll know it was me. Brian doesn't have anyone else who cares as much as I do."

She showed him to the door, shook his hand solemnly. He said he'd be in touch as soon as he had something to report; she said, "I'll pray for him"—not quite a non sequitur. As soon as he was outside, she retreated into the world she occupied behind closed doors—devout Christian world, black woman's world, mother's world.

The Ford needed gas; he stopped at a service station at the top of Twin Peaks to fill the tank. His body needed food; he stopped at a Chinese restaurant on West Portal to fill his belly. One more time killer before he wrapped himself inside his empty apartment for the rest of the night—a stop at the Safeway on Taraval. He seldom ate in the apartment, kept little enough on hand, but one thing he did do regularly was brew a pot of tea. He was almost out of the Darjeeling blend Colleen had liked.

The store was Friday-night crowded. He was in the coffee and tea aisle, taking his time, reading labels, when a woman said, "Excuse me." The way she said it, as if the words had come out of only one side of her mouth, made him glance at her as he stepped back and she pushed by with her cart.

The first thing he focused on was the scarf. Tied funny under a Scottish style cap: down across the left side of her face, covering it entirely, and knotted under her chin. Only half of her mouth was visible. The right side of her face was oval, high-cheekboned, a thick-haired eyebrow bent in the middle like a snapped twig. Thirty-something. Attractive. Ash-blond hair showing beneath the cap. Body tightly encased in a black-and-white checked coat. That was all he registered before she was past him, without a glance in his direction. He watched her push the cart toward the checkstands up front, wondering a little about that scarf.

He picked out a package of tea, took it up to the quick-check. Misnomer tonight; there was a line and the checker was slow. Three stands over, the blond woman got through with her purchases before he did and was gone by the time he left the store.

His car was parked on Taraval, near Nineteenth Avenue. He headed that way, feeling twinges in his bad leg; cold had that effect sometimes. There was a small, covered parking lot on that side of Safeway, and he was just starting past it when he heard the voices.

Man saying, "Come on, lady, show my buddy here."

Woman saying, "Leave me alone."

Another man saying, "Just one look, I never seen somebody with half a face before."

Runyon paused to look over there. The blond woman in the scarf. The two males had her backed up against one of the slant-parked cars, crowding her. Late teens—he could see them plainly in the floodlights. She was holding her grocery sacks up high in front of her chest, like shields. He heard her say, "Please, just leave me—" before the bigger of the two suddenly reached up and tore the scarf away from her face.

She cried out, dropped one of the sacks—it broke apart on the concrete, scattering the contents—and tried to pull away, her free hand pawing at the scarf. The entire left side of her face had a frozen, twisted look; her mouth might have been split in half, one side normal, the other bent and the lip curled up over her teeth. One of the kids said, "Hey, man, didn't I tell you?" and the other one laughed like a hyena, and by then Runyon was on them.

He caught the big one by the shoulder of his denim jacket and yanked him aside, at the same time giving the other a hard push in the chest. That freed the woman; he heard her heels beating on the pavement as she ran out of harm's way. His attention was on the two teenagers.

One of them said, "What the fuck's the idea?" Spiked hair, pimples, straggly chin whiskers. The bigger one— buzz cut and longer whiskers—just glared. Runyon knew the type. Bullies. Tough on the outside, mush on the inside. Not dangerous unless they were cornered or thought they had the upper hand.

"I could ask you the same question."

"You want a piece of us, man?" the other one said.

"You want a piece of a jail cell?"

"Huh?"

"You heard me."

"Christ, Curt, he's a cop."

The shorter one put his hands up, palms outward. "Hey, man, we weren't doing anything. Just having a little fun, that's all."

"If hassling a woman is your idea of fun, you're pretty damn stupid. Go on, get out of here. But I'll remember both of you. I hear about you hanging around here hassling anybody again, you won't like what happens."

They went. Looking back over their shoulders at him, muttering to one another. He watched them out of sight, uphill on Taraval, before he looked for the woman.

She'd gone to the far end of the parking area, up against the shrub-topped retaining wall on the Eighteenth Avenue side. Now, hesitantly, she came back toward him, still carrying the one grocery sack. The scarf, he saw, had been retied to cover the left side of her face. When she stopped near him, she stood in a half-turned posture, her right side toward him.

"You okay, miss?"

"Yes. Thank you."

"Kids these days. No sense of decency."

"I'm used to it," she said flatly.

"Used to it?"

No answer to that. Instead she bent and began picking up the spilled groceries one-handed. Runyon said, "Here, let me help," and took the second sack and refilled it, crawling halfway under one of the parked cars to retrieve a can of soup. "Looks like that's everything."

"Thank you again."

"Your car in here?"

"I can manage."

"I don't mind. Heavy cans in this bag."

She hesitated, shrugged. "At the back wall."

He followed her to where one of those small, box-shaped Scions that look like recycled postal delivery vans was slanted. Chocolate-colored, which made it even uglier. She keyed open the trunk, set the one sack inside, waited while he put the other one beside it. When he straightened he was close to her, close to the uncovered side of her face. And what he saw in that one eye, clearly visible in the trunk light and floodlights, shocked him.

He was looking at pain.

He'd seen pain in another woman's eyes not long ago, a woman who resembled Colleen, but it was nothing like this. This was raw and naked, the kind that goes marrow-deep, soul-deep. The kind that had stared back at him from his mirror throughout Colleen's illness and in all the days since her death.

"If you're done staring," she said, "I'd like to leave now."

"I'm sorry, I . . ."

"Don't be. I told you, I'm used to it."

She slammed the trunk lid, and without looking at him again she got into the car and backed it up and left him standing there alone, the glimpses he'd had of her face and her pain still sharp in his mind.

4

The kinds of things women will talk about to each other, casually, in public places and in front of men, never cease to amaze me. There doesn't seem to be any subject matter too personal, too outrageous for discussion.

Cosmetic surgery, for instance.

Intimate cosmetic surgery.

Nip and tuck the likes of which I couldn't have dreamed up in my wildest fantasies.

Friday night I found out far more than I ever wanted to know about this topic. And in the unlikeliest of places—over dinner in a moderately expensive, sedate Italian restaurant in Ghirardelli Square.

The two women in question were Kerry and Tamara. Since my semiretirement, and even more since her struggles with breast cancer, Kerry and I had been spending a lot more time together. She was cancer-free again, after months of radiation therapy, but she was still taking medication and still working through the psychological effects, and she would need regular six-month checkups for the rest of her life because there was always the chance that cancerous cells could recur. Time had become a major factor in both our lives. A cancer scare coupled with advancing age makes you aware of how little time you may have left and how important it is to make every minute you have together count. So we did family things with Emily, and on at least one weekend day or night the two of us went to restaurants, movies, plays, the symphony at Davies Hall, the new de Young Museum, a 49ers game at the 'Stick.

It had been Kerry's idea to invite Tamara to join us for dinner at Bella Mia. Tamara hadn't been getting out much since her long-time, cello-playing boyfriend, Horace, who had moved east for a year's gig with the Philadelphia Philharmonic, decided to play permanent bedroom music with another woman. There was nobody new in her life. By her admission and complaint, she hadn't gotten laid since Horace left ten months ago—a tragedy of large proportions for a hormone-rich twenty-six-year-old. Added to all this was the fact that her best friend, Vonda, had turned up pregnant and was about to be married. She'd become a little reclusive away from the agency, and sometimes moody and mopey and grumbly at work. Kerry thought an evening with us might cheer her up, which I considered a dubious notion. I expected Tamara to decline the invitation, but she jumped at it. Good sign. Maybe it meant she was tired of the shell she'd crawled into and was ready to break out. Why else would she want to hang with a couple old enough to be her parents, if not her grandparents?

So there we were at Bella Mia, in a corner booth, sharing

a bottle of good Chianti and chatting along comfortably about general subjects while we tucked into steaming bowls of minestrone. And then Kerry made the mistake, in my opinion anyway, of asking Tamara about Vonda's wedding plans. This led into the nip and tuck business.

"You'll never guess what Ben's giving her for a wedding present," Tamara said. "Gummy bears."

I said in my naïve way, "Candy? What kind of wedding present is that?"

She laughed. "Not those kind of gummy bears."

"What other kind is there?"

Kerry said, "That doesn't say much for Ben."

"No, it wasn't his idea, it was Vonda's. He's cool with her just the way she is, but she's always hated being a C cup."

"Well, you know, pregnancy can sometimes increase size."

"Probably won't in her case. Doctor says she can't nurse."

"That's too bad. Still, gummy bears haven't been proven completely safe."

I said, "What are you talking about? What're gummy bears?"

"Breast implants," Kerry said.

"New kind of silicon material," Tamara said, "supposed to look and feel like the candy. You know, soft and gooey."

I made a fast reach for my glass of wine.

"Maybe I'm just being alarmist," Kerry said, "but after what I've been through, I wouldn't allow any kind of foreign matter in my breasts."

"Mine are saggy enough as it is. Wouldn't want my nipples messed with, either."

"Absolutely not."

"My booty lifted, now, I could go for that."

"Oh, there's nothing wrong with your booty."

"Not what my mirror tells me when I get out of the shower."

"A woman I work with at Bates and Carpenter had an umbilicoplasty. Can you believe it?"

"Belly button, right?"

"Right. She had an inny and always wanted an outie."

"I can relate to that. How'd it turn out?"

"She showed it off at the office. Looked fine, you couldn't tell a thing."

"Girl I know had her nose done about a year ago. Really made a difference in her appearance."

"You see a lot of rhinoplasties these days."

"Rhinoplasty," I said. "Sounds like a horn job on a zoo animal."

They ignored me. Tamara said, "That's one thing I don't need. Maybe a lipo, though, lose the fat roll around my middle."

"It wouldn't be worth it," Kerry said. "Having a tube stuck in you, being hooked up to a machine that sucks like a vacuum cleaner . . . no, thank you. Messy, painful, and there's a long recuperative period."

"Yeah, you're right. Nasty."

"A face-lift is no picnic, either, I'm told."

"Lot of downtime, right?"

"Yes, but you only look like an accident victim for the first few days. Anyhow, it's not something you'll need to consider for a lot of years yet."

"You either."

"Thanks, that's a sweet lie. I should have my eyes done, at least."

"What's the matter with your eyes?" I said.

"Not the eyes themselves. The bags and hen's feet."

"The what?"

"Make you look and feel great, I'll bet," Tamara said.

"I know it would."

We ate and drank a little in blessed silence. But not for long. "That labia surgery," Tamara said, "you heard about that? Got to be pretty nasty, too. I wouldn't want anybody cutting me up down there."

"Labiaplasty. My God, no."

Foolishly I asked, "What's labiaplasty?"

"You don't really want to know."

"Sure I do. What is it?"

"Okay," Kerry said, "you asked for it. It's cosmetic re-configuration of the outer labia of the vagina."

I sat there for about ten seconds before I said, "You're right, I didn't really want to know."

"Supposed to be for beautification purposes," Tamara said, "get rid of the droop."

Droop? *Droop?*

"But why would you bother? I mean, nobody's gonna be looking down there but you, and even if some guy did look, he wouldn't know the difference."

"That's for sure."

Tamara said dreamily, "One thing I can see myself getting talked into, that's the hymen reattachment thing."

"You're kidding. You wouldn't, would you?"

"Need all the help with my sex life I can get. Lot of guys love to think they're getting a virgin."

"Don't they, though."

I almost choked on a mouthful of wine over this exchange.

Tamara was watching me. She smiled her Evil Tamara smile. "Women aren't the only ones having stuff like this done. Guys, too."

"That's right," Kerry said. "There's manscaping, for instance."

"There's *what*?" I said.

"Manscaping. Having body hair waxed or lasered off."

"The new seal look," Tamara said. "Very cool."

My God.

"Then there's pectoral implants."

"And six-pack tummy tucks."

"And testicle tucks."

"And penis enhancement, for livin' large."

"And male breast reduction."

"And uncircumcisions."

I put down my wineglass. Carefully. "You made that last one up."

"No," Kerry said, "she didn't."

"How the hell can a man have himself *un*circumsised?"

"It's called foreskin reconstruction. Very trendy among the younger set, I understand."

"Bull."

"Tamara?"

"Fact," she said. "Lot of dudes think it's cool. Some even having their new foreskin tattooed."

What can you say to that? True or false, it absolutely defies comment.

I just sat there, silent, looking back and forth from one to the other as they cheerfully chattered on about chemical peels and laser resurfacing and hyperpigmentation removal and buttock augmentation and hyperbaric oxygen therapy, and how twenty-five percent of all cosmetic surgeries were mother-daughter tandems, and how nose jobs and chin lifts were the hot new gifts for wealthy parents to give to their kids on high school and college graduation, and which Hollywood celebs were being sucked, tucked, lifted, reconstructed, and resurfaced by which Hollywood celeb surgeon—all the while eating minestrone and salad and garlic bread and drinking wine with plenty of appetite, the kind I'd had when I sat down in the booth with them and might never have again.

Alone with Kerry on the way home, I said, "All that cosmetic surgery nonsense. The two of you were putting me on, right? At least about some of the more personal procedures?"

"Why would you think that?"

"I can't believe people would have things like that done to themselves."

"You can say that after, what, forty years as a detective? People are capable of doing *anything* to themselves. And others."

I couldn't argue with that. "So those procedures really do exist? All of them?"

"Every one."

"How come you and Tamara know so much about it?"

"Word of mouth, for one thing."

"Women's mouths."

"Don't be sexist," she said. "We also read newspapers and surf the Net, two things you don't do. You'd be amazed at what you can find out if you take a ride on the information highway."

"Information highway," I said. "Surf the Net."

"Stuck in the past. Living with blinders on."

"Okay, okay. But I still don't get it."

"Get what?"

"The whole cosmetic surgery bit. Women want to look younger, sure, I understand that. Vanity. But the rest of it . . . unnatural, demeaning, seems to me. Ways for some fat-cat surgeon to get rich."

"It's not vanity. Not completely, anyway."

"Then what is it?"

"A kind of celebration of life in general and our bodies in particular. Life is short and the body wears out fast—and the medical community is making huge advances in all areas, including cosmetic surgery. Why not preserve and resurface, if you can afford to, the parts only you or an intimate partner see as well as the parts everyone else sees?"

"Don't tell me you're thinking about having yourself resurfaced?"

"As a matter of fact, I am."

Oh, God. "What kind of procedure? Not a face-lift . . ."

"Why not a face-lift?"

"I like your face just fine the way it is."

"Well, I don't. Maybe not a full lift, maybe just my eyes and Botox or collagen injections around my mouth and chin. Get rid of the hen's feet and some of the wrinkles."

"What if something went wrong? You could end up scarred or disfigured . . ."

"Oh, come on. Cosmetic surgery is completely safe."

"You said yourself it's no picnic."

"Neither were the radiation treatments. If I could get through them, I can get through anything."

"I still don't like the idea of it."

"You're not going to give me any trouble if I decide to go ahead, are you?"

". . . No. Your body, your decision."

"Now that's the most enlightened thing you've said all evening. If you really mean it, and if I do go ahead, I might include a little present in the package."

"Present? What present?"

"Reattachment of a certain membrane, just for you."

5

JAKE RUNYON

Tamara had e-mailed him some preliminary background information on Brian Youngblood; he looked it over on his laptop Friday night, after he got back to the apartment. First thing you always checked for when somebody was in trouble was a criminal record of any kind, adult or juvenile. Youngblood had neither one. Not even a misdemeanor driving infraction.

One possible in his credit history. There was a state law prohibiting private detectives and other citizens from using credit-monitoring services like TRW for investigative purposes; but realtors could subscribe to these services, since they were in the buying and selling business, and the agency had an arrangement with one in their former office building on O'Farrell Street. Runyon didn't know the nature of the arrangement. Not his business.

According to Youngblood's mother, Brian was very

good at his profession and made a good salary. According to the credit report, he'd spent most of the past sixteen months mired in debt. Credit cards maxed to the limit, with not even the minimum paid. Two and three months in arrears on his rent; an eviction notice had been issued and then rescinded when he came up with the three-month balance. PG&E and telephone bills unpaid and service shut off twice by Pac Bell. The crisis point had been reached at the end of August. Might've been forced to declare bankruptcy if he hadn't come into a windfall of at least ten thousand dollars. This allowed him to pay off everything he owed and to reestablish his credit.

But the fix had been only temporary. In the ninety days since, he'd managed to shove himself right back into a money trap at an accelerated rate: credit cards nearly maxed out, rent and utility bills upaid. If he didn't do something about the new crisis, he was bound to go under this time.

Did his mother know where the ten thousand had come from? Probably not. Likely didn't know anything about it at all or she'd've mentioned it. Something in that, maybe.

Something, too, in what had put Youngblood in the credit crunch in the first place. Until sixteen months ago, he'd had a fairly stable credit rating. No clue in the rest of his personal history.

There were two ways to handle a case like this. One was to talk to the subject first, worry him a little, and see if he could be made to own up to his problem. The other was to talk to his friends and neighbors and coworkers, find out what they knew, and try to build up a clear picture of the situation before you braced the subject. Runyon preferred the direct approach whenever possible, and that seemed to be the best way to go here, particularly since he had no address yet for Youngblood's friend Aaron Myers. No listing for Myers in the phone directory. Tamara could turn up his address and the name of his employer easily enough on Monday, but that was Monday and this was Friday night and the weekend stretched out ahead.

No need for him to wait until Monday. He'd told Rose Youngblood he would start the investigation today and he was a man who kept his word. Saturday was just another workday. Just another twenty-four hours in the string of days that made up what was left of his life.

Brian Youngblood lived on Duncan Street, on the downhill side of Diamond Heights just above Noe Valley. Elderly wood-and-stucco building that contained four good-sized flats, judging from its size; Youngblood's was one of those on the upper floor, south side, which meant views of the southern curve of the city and the bay beyond. Doing fairly well for himself, all right. Rents in the city, in a neighborhood like this, didn't come cheap.

Runyon found a place to park and climbed the high front stoop. There were two doors, set at right angles, on either side of a narrow vestibule, each with its own bell button. The labels on the bank of mailboxes told him Youngblood's flat number was 3; he leaned on the bell.

It was a windy late fall day, clouds chasing one another across the sky to the east; Runyon pulled his coat collar up against the chill. Out on the bay a freighter from the Port of Oakland was moving slowly under the arch of the Bay

Bridge, heading toward the Gate. He watched it while he waited. Colleen had always wanted to take a vacation cruise on a freighter, in the days when you could still book passage on one—down through the Panama Canal to the Caribbean. Another cruise she'd tried to talk him into was on one of the luxury ships that went up the Inside Passage to Ketchikan, Juneau, and other ports along the Alaskan coast.

No answer. He pressed the bell again.

But shipboard travel wasn't his idea of a good time. Too confining, too regimented. He'd put her off, made excuses, steered her into other, landlocked vacations that allowed him freedom of movement. Selfish. She'd never said anything, she was never one to complain or wheedle or argue, but she must have been disappointed. Someday we'll do it, he'd said. Only someday never came, not for either of them. Every time he thought about it, he felt like a shit for having denied her a simple pleasure that would have made her life, while she still had a life, a little happier.

Still no answer.

One thing he knew now, anyway: Youngblood wasn't hurt badly enough to stay at home on a Saturday morning.

He decided he might as well see what, if anything, Dré Janssen could tell him. He drove to Chestnut Street in the Marina, wasted nearly half an hour hunting up a legal parking space, and got exactly nothing for the effort. Janssen didn't work on Saturdays. Neither of the two clerks on duty in the video store could or would tell him where the manager lived.

Neither could the phone directory. Everybody had unlisted

numbers these days, it seemed—hunger for what little privacy remained to the average citizen in the Big Brother age.

One more thing that would have to wait until Monday.

Long drive down the spine of the Peninsula on Skyline Boulevard, a swing over to the coast, a grilled cheese sandwich in Half Moon Bay, and back into the city on Highway 1.

Another pass by the Duncan Street address. Brian Youngblood still wasn't home. Or he was home and not answering his doorbell.

The hell with it. Tomorrow was another day to fill up, get through.

On his way to the apartment, he saw the woman in the scarf again.

It was after six and he was stopped at the Taraval light on Nineteenth Avenue. He chanced to glance over just as she was coming out of the coffee shop on the southwestern corner. Same black-and-white checked coat, different-colored scarf, but tied in the same way over the left side of her face. Her, no doubt of it. She was walking away to the west when the light changed.

He drove three blocks before impulse made him turn and loop back around to Taraval. By the time he crossed Nineteenth, she was nowhere in sight. No sign of the chocolate-colored Scion, either. One more pass around, same results, before he gave it up and drove on to Ortega.

Just as well. What would he have done if she'd still been there? What could he say to her?

Crazy coincidence, that was all it was. You live in a big city neighborhood, you can go months or years without seeing the same person twice. So she occupied space somewhere in his neighborhood, so what? He'd probably never see her a third time. Didn't matter if he did, did it?

Not in the long run, no, but it seemed to matter right now. Seeing her again had put her in the forefront of his mind. Her, and the intense pain that had radiated from her good eye the night before. That was why he'd given in to the impulse. Drawn to pain and suffering, like a moth to candle fire. Colleen. Risa Niland, who resembled Colleen, whose sister had been brutally murdered. Drawn to their hurt and then ultimately repelled by it because it was the same as his own and there was nothing he could do to ease it, much less put an end to it.

He'd let himself believe there might be a way with Risa Niland, given himself a little taste of false hope, and what had that got him? Nothing. When an opportunity came to pursue it, he hadn't been able to make the first move. She might've been receptive if he had; the timing was right for her, if not him. But it wouldn't have worked out if he had. A Colleen substitute was the last thing he wanted or needed.

Forget the woman in the scarf. She was nobody to him, just one more among the legion of sufferers. Probably married anyway, couple of kids, a job, a life. The left side of her face . . . accident, disease, whatever. Bad things happen to people all the time. He knew that if anybody did. None of his business. Forget it.

But that one good eye, dammit.

Like something burning . . .

6

TAMARA

She was alone in the offices when the woman came stumbling in.

Monday morning, a little after nine. Bill wasn't due in today and Jake and Alex were out on field assignments. Quiet; the phone hadn't even rung yet. Some days, she enjoyed being here by herself. In control, the nerve and brain center of the agency. Nerve and brain center—the phrase made her smile.

Shaping up to be a better Monday than most, all right. Weather was good, bright and sunny. And she'd had a pretty nice weekend for a change. Dinner with Kerry and Bill on Friday night—she grinned, remembering the look on Bill's face during the rap about cosmetic surgery. New apartment hunting again yesterday; still hadn't found a place that had everything she wanted—location, size, view—but she always had a good time looking. And then dinner with sister Claudia and her Oreo lawyer boyfriend, and for once neither of them had been obnoxious. Good day all around.

Who needed a man in her life? Well, she did, at least for a night now and then (God, she was horny!), but not having somebody didn't bother her as much as it had after that fool chump Horace dumped her. She had a good life other than her love life and she was finally learning how to enjoy it on its own terms.

She finished her first cup of coffee while she answered a couple of phone messages, went out into the anteroom for a refill from the hot plate. Sunlight streamed in through the windows facing South Park. So did a fair amount of filtered noise. Lot of activity in and around the Park these days. The neighborhood had been the hub of the dot-com boom in the eighties and early nineties; now, a decade after the collapse of the market, it had bounced back with a vengeance. Web 2.0 companies were moving back in in droves—must be close to a dozen now—and South Park was once more "the town square of Multimedia Gulch."

Thinking about that made her feel good, too. She and Bill had swung a sweet long-term lease on this building when the real estate market was in the tank; couldn't afford the going rent if they were trying to buy in now. And the high-tech companies being so close meant the likelihood of more business. The agency hadn't gotten much out of the dot-com industry to date, but that could change. Web 2.0 companies had their employee and security problems same as any other big business, and when they did, the odds were favorable they'd hire a firm that happened to be in their own backyard.

Tamara poured her cup full, stirred in some low-cal sweetener, and went back into her office. She was just sitting down when she heard the anteroom door open. Jake or Alex, probably. She didn't bother to turn around for a look—not until the door slammed hard and there was a loud scraping sound as if the person out there was shoving furniture around. A woman's voice called, "Hello? Anybody here?" That put her on her feet and sent her over to the door.

Lord!

The woman must have lurched against the couch; it was canted out from the wall and she was leaning on the back of it, bent over, her face turned sideways so that she seemed to be looking up from under, in Tamara's direction. Bad news. Big lemon-colored bruise on the left side under the eye, cuts and swelling on the right cheekbone, puffed lip, more cuts and scrapes on the chin. No blood, dried or otherwise, on her face. No blood on the jacket, blouse, or jeans she wore. The pounding she'd taken was at least a day old.

Tamara registered all of that before she recognized the woman.

"Remember me?"

"Janice Krochek. What happened to you?"

Krochek didn't answer. She sank onto the couch, sat with elbows resting on her knees. Pale, sweaty. Exhausted. Tense, too, the way she'd been in the Hillman last week. And scared. Trying to hide it behind a half smile and a flip tone, but her eyes gave her away; the scare was big and wormy in them.

"Who did that to you, Mrs. Krochek?"

"Nobody did it. I fell down some stairs."

Yeah, sure.

"You wouldn't have anything to drink, would you? Bourbon, Scotch?"

"Just coffee and water."

"I thought all private detectives kept a bottle of booze around."

"Yeah, well, that's crap. This is a business office."

"All right, coffee. Lots of cream and sugar. How about a cigarette?"

"Nobody here smokes."

"Figures. Aspirin? My head hurts like hell."

Tamara went and got the tin of aspirin from her purse, poured the coffee. She had to open the tin herself; Krochek's hands were too shaky. The woman slurped down four of them. Inside of her mouth must've been cut; she made a face and dribbled coffee out of the side with the puffed lip.

"You need a doctor," Tamara said.

"No. No doctor. I'm all right."

"You don't look all right."

"I walked all the way here. Fifteen goddamn blocks."

"Why? Why'd you come here?"

"No place else to go."

"What about your friend?"

"I don't have any friends." Bitterly.

"Woman you're staying with, Ginger Benn."

"Not staying there anymore."

"Why not? Because you got beat up?"

Slurp, slurp. She was holding the cup in both hands, tight and up close to her face, alternately slurping and breathing in the steam like an asthmatic. Marks on both wrists, too, Tamara saw then—red chafe marks.

She said, "So you remembered the business card we left last week. South Park—easy address to remember."

"I don't know what I'd've done if I hadn't. Where's your boss? Not here?"

"No. And he's not my boss."

"Lover?"

"Business partner," Tamara said.

"You're kidding."

"Do I look like I'm kidding?"

"Black—white, May—December. What kind of partnership is that?"

Tamara bit back the sharp retort that crawled out on her tongue. The woman was hurt; you couldn't tell a beating victim to go fuck herself, even one as snotty as this one. Not yet, anyway.

"Why don't you tell me who beat you up, Mrs. Krochek?"

"Nobody beat me up. I told you, it was an accident."

"Accident with somebody's fist. Like maybe Carl Lassiter?"

"No."

"Because of the money you owe him or his boss?"

"I said no. Accident, accident—how many times do you want to hear it?"

Could be Lassiter she was afraid of, could be somebody else. Tamara couldn't tell with Krochek's eyes cast downward and steam from the coffee smearing her expression.

"What do you care anyway?" Krocheck said.

"I don't like to see anybody get beat up. Women especially."

"It's none of your business."

"You're in my offices, that makes it my business. Police business, too. Assault is a felony."

The word "police" seemed to scare Krochek even more. "I wasn't assaulted! I don't want anything to do with the law, you understand?"

"Yeah, I understand. Just why'd you come here?"

"Didn't I just tell you that, too? I didn't have any place else to go."

"What do you want us to do for you?"

"Get me home."

"Oakland Hills?"

"Where the hell else. That's the only home I've got—for now anyway. Can I have some more coffee? More sugar this time."

What am I, Tamara thought, some kind of servant? Fetch this, fetch that. Yassum, Miz Scarlett. Grumbling to herself, she went and got the refill. When she brought it back, she said, "So you changed your mind after all. Now you want to go back to your husband."

"Woman's prerogative."

"If you weren't coerced into it."

"It's changed, isn't that enough? Enough questions! Can't you see I'm hurting?"

"Offered to get you a doctor."

"I don't want a doctor. I want to go home."

"So why didn't you call your husband, have him come get you?"

"With what? I don't have my cell anymore. No money, either. Why do you think I walked all the way over here?"

"Where's your purse?"

Shrug.

"Whoever beat on you take it?"

Slurp.

"You could've called from Ginger's room, or the lobby desk."

Krochek winced, pressed fingers gingerly against her puffed lip. "For God's sake. Will you just call Mitch for me? Will you do that, please?"

Tamara said with sour irony, "Quicker the better," and went into her office to make the call.

But getting rid of Janice Krochek wasn't going to be that easy. Her husband was away from Five States Engineering today, out on some job site. Tamara pried his cell number out of Krochek's assistant, but when she called it she got his voice mail. She left a curt message, saying it was urgent he return the call as soon as possible.

Back to the anteroom, where she found Janice Krochek curled up in a fetal position on the couch. Sound asleep, making little wheezing, moaning noises in her nose and throat. She'd spilled some of the coffee on the low table and carpet and hadn't bothered to wipe it up.

Oh, yeah, great. Terrific. Just what the agency needed for an advertisement if a client should happen to walk in— a banged-up gambling junkie passed out on the anteroom couch.

Krochek had shed her coat; it was crumpled on the floor. Tamara picked it up, started to drape it over the woman, and then hesitated. Might as well play detective here, just for practice. She ran her a hand into each of the pockets. One was empty; the other had the agency business card Bill had left for her, and a folded piece of paper torn off a scratch pad. Written in ink on the paper, in a woman's hand, was: *La Farge—s. 1408.* Below that, heavily underlined several times, was the numeral 9.

One of her johns, or something to do with the money she owed? Not that it mattered; once she was out of here, the agency was through with her and her messed-up life. Tamara put the paper back where she'd found it, spread the coat over the lower half of Krochek's body. The woman didn't move, just kept right on snoring.

She sighed. So much for another try at the woman-to-woman thing. And so much for the good mood she'd been in earlier.

She got a towel and cleaned up the coffee spill, washed out the used mug. In her office, waiting for the phone to ring, she answered a couple of e-mails and tracked down an address Jake needed for the pro bono case and then called him on his cell. Voice mail again. Whole damn world was unavailable this morning, it seemed. She left him a message.

An hour passed. Still no callback from Mitchell Krochek. She went out to check on the woman. Hadn't moved, from the look of her. Her breathing was still noisy and a little labored.

Well, shit.

Tamara called Bill's home number. Answering machine. So then she called his cell. If she got his voice mail, too . . .

She didn't. He answered on the third ring. She said, "I hate to bother you but I've got a problem here," and explained about her sweetheart morning with the Fever Woman.

"She would have to pick on us," Bill said. "Unpredictable as hell, that's the trouble with addicts."

"Probably shouldn't've taken the case in the first place."

"Hindsight, the great teacher."

"So what do I do? Keep on waiting for her husband to call back?"

"No. He might not check his messages."

"She can't sleep or hang here all day. I've got a client coming in for a consultation at one o'clock."

"Where's Jake?"

"Busy. He's not answering his cell and Alex is down in San Jose. I suppose I could cancel the appointment and close up, take her over to Oakland myself . . ."

"You've had enough hassle already. I'll do it."

"You sure? If you're busy . . ."

"Busy doing nothing," he said. "Errands, that's all. It'll take me twenty minutes or so to get to South Park. If Krochek calls in the meantime, give him my cell number and I'll work something out with him."

Bet he doesn't call, she thought.

He didn't.

7

Janice Krochek was still sleeping on the anteroom couch when I got there. She'd been pretty badly used, all right. Looking down at her built an impotent anger in me. Violence against women infuriates me every time I encounter it. Nobody, no matter how much they mess up their own lives, deserves to become somebody's punching bag.

"She won't see a doctor," Tamara said. "Just wants to go home."

"Maybe her husband can talk her into it."

"If he cares enough. I'll tell him when he calls, if he calls."

"She told you she walked here?"

"That's what she said. Benn woman threw her out, apparently, wouldn't even let her use the phone."

"That doesn't sound right."

"Didn't to me, either. Why didn't she ask the desk clerk or one of the other residents?"

"Maybe it wasn't the Hillman she walked from."

"Fifteen blocks, she said."

"It's a wonder she made it that far in her condition. And without anybody stopping to help her."

"In this city?" Tamara said. "Army of *Dawn of the Dead* zombies could march up Market Street and nobody'd pay much attention."

"Yeah. Come on, let's wake her up. I'm parked in a loading zone across the Square."

Together we hoisted Janice Krochek into a sitting position. Tamara shook her a little until one bleary eye popped open and focused on me. "You," she said.

"Me," I agreed. "How do you feel?"

"Groggy. Shitty."

"I can take you to a hospital, get you some medical attention . . ."

"No. Home." The other eye was open now; her gaze roamed from side to side. "Where's Mitch?"

"We couldn't get hold of him," I said. "He's on a job site today."

"Yeah, sure. Out screwing his latest bimbo."

"Come on, Mrs. Krochek, on your feet. I'll take you home."

We got her upright. Shaky, but she could stand and move all right with my hand on her arm; I didn't need Tamara's help to get her downstairs. A couple of people on the sidewalk and in the park strip gave us passing glances and a wide berth.

One of South Park's many attractions is that a Bay Bridge approach is only a short distance away. We were on the bridge in five or six minutes. Janice Krochek sat slumped in the seat, her eyes closed, massaging her chafed wrists, unresponsive to the questions I put to her. Whoever had beat her up, for whatever reason, she wasn't about to confide to me. Or, I'd have been willing to bet, to her husband.

She was asleep again by the time we came off the bridge. I woke her up with a couple of sharp words to get directions; I had the Krocheks' home address but the street name wasn't familiar and I wasn't going to stop to pore over a map. "Highway 24," she said, "then straight up Claremont, ask me again when you pass the Claremont Hotel."

My cell phone went off at about the time we reached the Claremont. Had to be Tamara. I pulled over to answer it; unlike most people nowadays, I don't consider talking on the phone while driving to be safe, and it's even less so on narrow, hilly streets.

Tamara said, "Mr. Krochek just called. I gave him the news. He'll meet you at his house—on his way there right now."

"Reaction?"

"Relieved and pissed off."

I relayed the message to Janice Krochek, omitting the relieved and pissed off part.

"Be still, my heart," she said.

We kept climbing. Turn right on this street, left on that one, half a mile and then right again on such-and-such. By then we were well up into the hills. Panoramic views of the bay, San Francisco, three bridges, Alcatraz Island. Expensive living for the financially well-endowed.

What was surprising about the area was how quickly it

had been regenerated, how many new homes had sprung from the ashes of the firestorm that had engulfed these hills in October of 1991. Hardly any signs remained of the devastation along the narrow, winding roads. High winds, brush-clogged canyons, and tinder-dry trees had spawned that fire, and before it was done raging it had reached temperatures as high as two thousand degrees Fahrenheit, hot enough to boil asphalt, burned sixteen hundred acres, destroyed nearly three thousand single-family homes and apartment buildings, left twenty-five people dead, and caused something like a billion and a half dollars in damage.

The Krocheks were too young to have lived up here at that time; they were among the multitude of newcomers who had figured lightning would never strike twice and so bought themselves a chunk of the rebuilt, relandscaped, million-dollar California Dream. They could have it. I preferred the West Bay; despite all its civic and other problems and the lurking threat of the Big One, the predicted earthquake disaster that would make the Oakland Hills fire look like a minor incident, San Francisco was my home and would be as long as I stayed above ground. My city, for better or for worse.

The Krocheks lived on Fox Canyon Circle, at the end of Fox Canyon Road—a rounded cul-de-sac like the bulb on top of a thermometer. It was backed up against one of the short, narrow canyons that threaded the area. Before the fire, these canyons had been clogged with oak, madrone, dry manzanita. Now, short grass and scrub grew down there and in places along the far bank you could see bare patches where the fire had burned and nothing had regrown.

Three large, Mediterranean-style homes, spaced widely apart, occupied the circle. The lower one on the north, away from the canyon, belonged to the Krocheks. The driveway was empty; Krochek hadn't got there yet. I pulled up in front. The house was set behind a low, gated stucco wall fronted by yew and yucca trees: tile roof, arched windows with heavy wood balconies and ornamental wrought iron trim. The white stucco gave off thin daggerish glints of midday sunlight.

At the middle house next door, slightly higher up, a woman wearing shorts and a dark green sun hat was doing some work in her low-maintenance, cactus-dominated front garden. She stopped and stood staring over at us, shading her eyes with one hand, as Janice Krochek and I got out. As soon as she recognized her neighbor, she started our way.

Janice Krochek said, "Oh, shit, just what I need. Rebecca."

I said, "Your husband should be here pretty soon."

"Do I care? I'm not going to wait around."

"How'll you get inside?"

"Spare key on the patio."

She started away, but she was still shaky on her pins. She faltered after a couple of steps, nearly fell. I went fast around the car and got hold of her arm. She said, "I'm all right," but she didn't try to pull away.

"Janice!"

The neighbor, Rebecca, came hurrying up. Mid-thirties, dark wavy hair under the sun hat, attractive in a long-faced, long-chinned way. It was windy and cool up here, not much of a November day for wearing shorts, but once I had a good look at her legs I knew she was the type who would wear them in the middle of a rainstorm. Long, tanned, beautifully shaped. Even a happily married old fart like me notices and appreciates fine craftsmanship.

Janice Krochek ignored her. Started forward again, dragging me with her. The neighbor changed direction so that she reached the drive just above us. "Janice, I thought you were gone for—" She broke off, her eyes going wide. "My God, your face . . . what happened to you?"

"Mind your own business, Rebecca."

"Do you need any help?"

"No."

"Mitch . . . does he know . . . ?"

"For Christ's sake, just leave me alone, will you?"

The dark-haired woman looked at me. I said, "We can manage, thanks," and let Mrs. Krochek lead me over to the gate in the fence, through it, and across a short tiled patio to the front entrance.

The spare key was under one of several decorative urns lined up along the wall; she told me which one and I got it for her and opened the door. She said, "Put it back where you found it." I said I would and while I was doing it, she disappeared inside—no thank you for my trouble, not another word.

I went back out through the gate. The neighbor was still standing in the driveway, waiting. She'd taken the sun hat off. She had a lot of hair piled up and pinned haphazardly, thick but very fine. Sunlight made the loose strands glisten like brown cornsilk.

I smiled and nodded and started around her, but she didn't let me finish the detour. She came over and put out a hand, not quite touching me. "I've never seen you before," she said. "Who are you?"

"A friend," I lied.

"Of whose? Hers?"

"Both."

"What happened to her?"

"An accident, she says. Fell down some stairs."

"Oh, crap. Somebody beat her up. Anyone can see that." I didn't say anything.

"Because of her gambling. Is that how you know her?" I didn't say anything.

"She's a compulsive gambler. You know that, don't you?"

I was moving again by then, completing the detour, but I didn't get halfway to my car before sudden noise put an end to the quiet. Motor, exhaust, and gearbox noise. A low-slung sports job, black and silver, came barreling along Fox Canyon Road and into the circle. Tires screeched as the driver braked and slid sideways into the driveway, forcing the neighbor and me to veer to one side.

Mitchell Krochek hopped out. Dark blue sports jacket and slacks, no tie, and a harried expression. He looked at me, looked at Rebecca, looked at me again. "Where is she?"

"In the house."

"All right?"

"Able to get around under her own power, but just barely. She ought to see a doctor."

"She hates doctors."

"See if you can get her to one anyway."

"Yeah, I'll do that." He looked at the neighbor again. "What're you doing here, Becky?"

"I was working in the garden when this man brought her home."

"Our neighbor, Rebecca Weaver," Krochek said to me. Not as if he were introducing her, as if he were apologizing for her showing up at the wrong place at the wrong time.

"I'd like to know what's going on," she said.

"So would I. I don't know."

"She's been beaten up, for God's sake. One of those people she associates with. What if they show up here?"

"That won't happen."

"It could. I'm here alone day and night, Mitch, I don't have to tell you that."

"Jesus," Krochek said. He looked and sounded half-angry, half-exasperated. "Nobody's going to bother you or Janice. Just go home, okay? I'll call you later if there's anything you need to know."

"Will you?"

"Yes, yes. Go on. Please."

The woman jammed her sun hat back on and went, reluctantly, with another distrustful glance in my direction. When she was out of earshot, Krochek said, "Divorced six months, not used to living alone. She got the house and a half-million-dollar settlement. If Janice divorces me, they'll be like two peas in fucking luxury pods and I'll be living in some rented apartment."

Nothing from me. I didn't want to get into that with him again.

"What happened to her?" he asked. "She tell you?"

"Wouldn't talk about it."

"No question it was a beating, though?"

"Not as far as I'm concerned. Judge for yourself when you see her."

"You think it was that guy you told me about, the enforcer . . . what's his name?"

"Lassiter. Could be."

"Or else some lowlife fellow gambler she hooked up with."

"Ask her. Maybe she'll tell you."

"Not if it's about gambling debts, more of my money down the sewer. And what the hell else could it be?" He raked fingers over one cheek, hard, the nails leaving reddish tracks in the skin. "Suppose he does show up here, the guy who beat her up? What am I supposed to do, pay him off?"

"That's up to you. If he trespasses, or makes overt threats in person or on the phone, call the police."

"The police. More hassle, more upheaval." He raked his cheek again. "Four years ago we were on top of the world, everything running smooth. Now it's a goddamn nightmare. I don't know how much more I can stand."

"She's back home," I said. "That's something."

"Yeah, but for how long? A week, a month, then it'll start all over again. I'm between a rock and a hard place—I can't live with her anymore, but if I let her divorce me I get a royal screwing. What the hell am I going to do?"

I didn't have any answers for him. He wasn't asking me, anyway.

A big battleship-shaped cloud floated across the sun and the gusting wind was suddenly chill. It made Krochek shiver, snapped him out of his bitter reverie. "I'd better get inside," he said. "Thanks for bringing Janice home. You didn't have to bother and I appreciate it. Let me pay you for your time . . ."

"Not necessary, Mr. Krochek. Just pay the invoice we sent you."

"Yes, I will, right away. Sorry about the delay. Sorry about what I said in the Ladderback last week, too, the crap about manufacturing evidence. I'm just not myself these days . . ." The words trailed off, blew away in the wind. He reached for my hand, shook it briefly, and trudged away up the drive, slump-shouldered, as if he were carrying a heavy weight on his back.

Lives you're glad you don't lead, people you wish well but hope you'll never see again.

8

JAKE RUNYON

It wasn't until late Monday afternoon that he finally caught up with Brian Youngblood.

He'd stopped by the Duncan Street address once on Sunday, and called Youngblood's number twice more, without getting any kind of response. Away from home or ducking visitors and callers—no way to tell which. Most of Monday had been taken up with more pressing work. He'd had time for one call to the home number that went unanswered. Duncan Street was more or less on Runyon's way to his apartment, so he made another pass by there shortly after five o'clock. And this time, his long lean on the doorbell produced results.

The intercom clicked, made noises like a hen laying an egg, and a staticky voice said warily, "Yes?"

"Brian Youngblood?"

Long pause. "Who is it?"

Runyon identified himself, said he was there at the request of Mrs. Rose Youngblood. No answer. Five seconds later the squawk box shut off. Thinking it over, maybe. He waited—two minutes, three. Then the intercom made chicken noises again.

"You still there, man?"

"I'm still here."

"All right. Come on up."

The door buzzed and Runyon went into a tiny foyer, then up a flight of carpeted stairs. Another door at the top swung open as he reached the landing. The young black man who stood peering at him through a pair of wire-rimmed glasses was thin, studious, with close-cropped hair that had already begun to recede. Nervous and ill at ease, too, but not necessarily for the same reason.

"Mr. Youngblood?"

Brief nod.

The business card Runyon handed over seemed to bemuse him, make him even more nervous. "A private investigator?" he said. Without benefit of intercom static, his voice was as thin as the rest of him. "You didn't say that's what you were. Why would my mother send a detective to see me?"

"She's concerned about you, the trouble you had last week. She thought I might be able to help."

"How can you help? It was just a—"

"Brian," a woman's voice called sharply from inside. "Don't talk out there—bring him in here."

Youngblood winced, a small rippling effect along one side of his face as if the voice had struck a nerve. His expression shifted, took on an almost hunted aspect. He was no longer making eye contact when he said, "We'd better go in."

Runyon followed him into a big, open front room. Heavy drapes had been drawn across the windows and the room was darkish as a result, palely lit by a desk lamp and a table lamp. Computer equipment dominated it—a workstation that took up one entire wall, not one terminal but two attached to a pair of twenty-two-inch screens, two printers, all sorts of other high-tech paraphernalia, and CD storage shelves. The rest of the furnishings were nondescript: an armchair, a recliner, a sofa, and some chrome-and-glass tables. The beige walls were empty of the kind of religious symbols his mother favored, of any other kind of picture or decoration.

A woman about Youngblood's age filled the armchair, lounging on her spine. The tall, lean, slinky type. Long, frizzy, tangled hair dyed a henna red that seemed wrong for her light brown skin tone. Spike heels and black net stockings and a green dress stretched tight across high breasts. The hard type, too: bright crimson lipstick, false eyelashes, too much eyeshadow and rouge.

Almost nothing surprised Runyon anymore, but Rose Youngblood had led him to believe her son's taste in women was conventional and conservative. This one was anything but. Neighbor, maybe?

Youngblood said, in a faintly embarrassed way, "This is Brandy. She's . . . a friend."

Brandy. Right.

Runyon nodded and said hello. Brandy gave him an

up-and-down glance, batted her eyelashes, and without taking her eyes off him, she said to Youngblood, "Who's he?" in a whiskey contralto—affected, not natural.

He went over and handed her Runyon's card. She looked at it and then made a little production of tucking it into the hollow between her breasts. "'Confidential investigator,' now isn't that something," she said. "Good-looking one, too, for a white man."

"Brandy, please . . ."

She mimicked him, "Brandy, please. Brandy, please. You're such a little pissant wimp."

"Don't say that. Why do you always have to get nasty?"

"You just don't want to hear the truth. Neither does that bible-thumping mama of yours." The purple-shaded eyes slid over Runyon again. "She really hire you to stick your nose into Brian's business?"

"The agency I work for, yes."

"Where'd she get the money? Old bitch gives every extra dime to that church of hers."

Runyon said nothing.

"Told her to mind her own business, didn't you?" she said to Youngblood. "Told her to just leave you alone."

"Yes, I told her."

"So why doesn't she listen to her little pussy-boy?"

Some piece of work, this one. Runyon had dealt with her type any number of times when he'd worked Vice on the Seattle PD. The tough, domineering, pseudo-sexual pose was calculated to push buttons, force you to play on her terms. All pure ego. The one thing her type couldn't stand was to be ignored.

He said to Youngblood, "What kind of trouble are you in, Brian?"

"You don't have to tell him anything," Brandy said.

"I'm asking you, not your friend."

Youngblood wouldn't look at him; his gaze was fixed on her. Runyon moved until he was standing between them.

"Don't stand in my way, sweetie."

"Talk to me," Runyon said to Youngblood. "There might be something I can do."

"My . . . my mother shouldn't have gone behind my back," Youngblood said. "I don't need a detective. I don't need anybody's help. It was an attempted carjacking, that's all."

"You told her you were mugged."

Brandy stirred in the chair but didn't get up. "Mugged, carjacked, what difference does it make?"

"Where did it happen? When?"

Headshake. You could see Youngblood trying to work up a lie. "Golden Gate Park," he said when he caught hold of one. "Near, uh, Stone Lake. Two guys. White guys. I didn't get a good look at them, it was too dark . . ."

"At night, then. And you were alone."

"That's right."

"What were you doing out there alone at night?"

"I, uh . . ."

"Leave the boy alone," Brandy said. Then, with a leer in her voice, "Come over here and talk to me instead."

"Why don't you tell me what really happened, Brian."

"I just told you . . ."

"The truth this time. Something to do with your friend here?"

"No."

"Your financial situation?"

". . . I don't know what you mean."

"Sure you do. Debts. Serious money crunch."

Brandy said, "Who the hell told you that?"

"How did you get in so deep?"

"Don't answer him. It's none of his fucking business."

"She have anything to do with it?" Runyon asked him.

"Brandy? No . . ."

"Where'd you get the ten thousand to bail you out in August?"

Youngblood said, "Oh, God."

Brandy said, "Come on now, leave the Mama's boy alone. Can't you see what a pussy he is?"

Runyon had had just about enough cheap Brandy. He said, "She's part of the trouble, all right. Any so-called friend with a mouth like hers is part of anyone's trouble."

"Ooo, I like a man talks hard like that. The harder the talk, the harder the dick. Hey, white meat. How about some *real* pussy right over here?"

"Cheap Brandy." He said it out loud, not trying to hide his contempt.

At first the phrase seemed to cut through the phony facade, kindle anger in her. Out of the corner of his eye he saw her start to lift herself out of the chair, the bloody lips peeled back away from her teeth. Something changed her mind; she sank back, her mouth twisting into a grimace. And then she began to laugh, a high, shrill sound that had no mirth in it.

"Is she the reason you got beat up?"

"No," Youngblood said. "I told you, she . . . it had nothing to do with her."

"But it wasn't a carjacking, and it didn't happen in the park."

Headshake.

"Come on, Mr. Youngblood. For your mother's sake."

Youngblood had moved so he could look at the woman. His eyes were pleading. "Brandy . . . ?"

She stopped laughing and said loudly, "No! To hell with her. You say one word to him and you'll regret it. I mean that, baby. You'll regret it!"

Now Youngblood looked scared as well as hunted and embarrassed. "You better leave, man," he said to Runyon.

"Is that what you want? You, not her."

"Yes. Yes."

"What do you want me to tell your mother?"

Brandy said, "Tell the Holy Roller to stay away from Brian. He doesn't need her, he doesn't need anybody but me."

"I'm sorry," Youngblood said. "Just tell her . . . I'm sorry."

Outside, Runyon sat in the Ford for a time, letting his tamped-down anger release before he did any more driving. The scene the three of them had just played kept running around in his head. Now that he was out of it, it seemed to have a vaguely surreal, vaguely ludicrous aspect, like Brandy herself. At the same time its hard and nasty edge hinted at all sorts of hidden tensions, hidden meanings.

She had some kind of hold on Youngblood—that seemed clear. Sex? Probably, but he had the feeling there was more to it than that. She seemed to hate his mother without even knowing her; if Rose Youngblood was aware of Brandy and her son's relationship with the woman, she'd have said so. So why the animosity on Brandy's part? And what was her connection to the beating he'd taken? Hell, maybe she was the one who'd done it. As hard and controlling as she seemed, she was capable of it.

The address Tamara had pulled up for Aaron Myers was a little over a mile from Duncan Street, in Noe Valley at the edge of the Mission District. Nondescript building with eight apartments that would be about half the size of Brian Youngblood's flat. Myers's was on the first floor, rear. Runyon rang the bell, waited, rang it again, waited some more.

Nobody home.

Dré Janssen? After five already. Bayside Video would be closed by the time he made it to Chesnut Street. Janssen and Myers could both wait until later. Rose Youngblood? She should be home by this time. No need to see her in person; he used his cell.

She answered almost immediately. He identified himself, listened to her voice turn flat when he told her he had nothing to report yet, just a more few questions.

"Have you heard from your son since we spoke on Friday?" he asked.

"No. I went to his apartment on Saturday, but he wasn't home."

"Did you go inside?"

"Of course not. I'm not that kind of parent. I respect my son's privacy."

"Do you know a woman friend of his named Brandy?"

"Brandy? No."

"He never mentioned the name?"

"I've never heard of anyone named Brandy."

"She seems to know you. Quite a bit about you, any-way."

"Brian must have told her. Who is she?"

"Not your son's usual kind of friend." He offered a cap-sule description without any of the details.

Hum on the line for a time before she said, "I had no idea Brian knew anyone as . . . coarse as that. I can't imag-ine why . . . oh." The last word was small and disapprov-ing. She'd just imagined why. But then she talked herself out of it by saying, "No, he'd wouldn't have anything to do with a woman like that. Not in that way. He's a good Christian, my son. No, absolutely not."

He let it go. Good mothers, particularly strongly reli-gious mothers, were unreliable witnesses. They almost always believed, no matter how much evidence was pre-sented to them, that their children were innocent creatures incapable of making the wrong choices, committing the kinds of sins they themselves would never dream of com-mitting.

He ate his dinner in the coffee shop on the corner of Nineteenth Avenue and Taraval. The woman with the scarf wasn't there; he hadn't expected her to be.

Hadn't expected to do what he did when he finished eating, either. Just went ahead and did it, without con-scious thought and against his better judgment, from some inner compulsion that he couldn't or wouldn't let himself identify.

He talked to both waitresses and a couple of customers, learned nothing, and then began canvassing the neighborhood for somebody who could tell him who she was.

9

Some days you'd be better off staying in bed with the covers pulled over your head.

You know the kind I mean. You wake up feeling out of sorts. The weather is lousy, cold and gray, and everything seems to be a source of irritation. Things like this happen: You cut yourself shaving, you squish barefoot into a deposit of strategically placed cat barf, little squabbles over nothing flare up to mar the normally comfortable breakfast-table atmosphere. Then you venture out into the damn city. Traffic seems heavier and some idiot cuts you off and one of the jet-propelled variety of lunatics runs a red light and nearly causes a collision. And then you arrive at the office and the day plunges downhill in earnest.

Wednesday was like that for me. Kerry calls Wednesdays hump days, a workplace term that means it's the middle of the week and once noon comes and goes, you're over the hump and heading for the weekend. This Wednesday was hump day, all right. In spades and with a whole new meaning to the term. Wednesday was the humper and I was the humpee.

Tamara had nothing to do with it; she was in a good mood and gave me no reason to growl at her personally. It was her answer to my simple question, "Any messages?" that provoked the initial growling and grumbling.

"Four," she said. "All from the same person, about every ten minutes since I got here at nine."

"And who would that be?"

"You're not going to like it."

"Then don't tell me."

"Mitchell Krochek," she said.

"You were right, I don't like it. What does he want now?"

"Wouldn't say. Wouldn't even leave you a voice mail. Just wants you to call him at his home number."

"His wife must've run off again."

"Well, he sounded pretty strung out."

"What does he expect us to do? We can't keep finding her and dragging her back every time she—"

The telephone cut me off.

"Want to bet who that is?" Tamara said.

When I got on the line, Krochek said, "Thank God. Man, I've been going crazy waiting here. Didn't your girl give you my message?"

"I just got in. And she's not my girl, she's my partner. She runs this agency."

"Yeah, right, sorry, I'm not thinking straight. Listen, something's happened. Can you come over here right away? My house?"

"What happened?"

"I don't know exactly, but it's bad. I don't want to talk about it on the phone."

I said, trying to keep the annoyance out of my voice, "Why not?"

"Something you have to see first."

"Look, Mr. Krochek . . ."

"I didn't know anybody else to call. I need help, your kind of help."

"Why don't you come over here and we'll talk about it—"

"No. It has to be *here*. As soon as possible." His voice kept climbing, loud enough so that I had to hold the receiver away from my ear. The raw edge of desperation in it sounded genuine. "I'll pay you five hundred dollars if you'll come right away. Will you? Please?"

I wanted to say no. I'd had enough of Krochek and his wife and their problems. Maybe I would have said no if I'd had morning appointments, pressing business, but my calendar was right there in front of me and there was nothing on it except routine business that I could deal with anytime. Besides, it was one of those days anyway, and I've always been a sucker for people in need. Heart full of mush, head full of rocks.

"Please?" Krochek said again. Begging now. The word had a moist sound.

"All right. But no promises for anything more than a few minutes' talk."

"That's all I ask. Right away?"

"As soon as I can get there."

He thanked me, twice. Then he said, "I'll have the five hundred in cash," and broke the connection.

I resisted an impulse to slam the receiver down. Tamara had been hanging around listening; she grinned at me from the connecting doorway.

"Don't say it," I said.

"Say what?"

"He offered me five hundred bucks for a brief conference. That's the only reason I'm going."

She laughed as if I'd said something funny.

Mitchell Krochek must have been waiting on his front patio; he opened the gate and stuck his head out as soon as I pulled into the driveway. He looked rumpled even from a distance: hair uncombed, floppy slippers on his feet, one tail of his shirt hanging out over a pair of faded Levi's. Up close, he had the bleary-eyed, saggy look that comes from too much alcohol and too little sleep. Anxiety showed plainly in his eyes. Something else, too: fear.

"I thought you'd changed your mind," he said.

It had taken me more than an hour and a half to make the drive. More annoyances: construction slowdown on the bridge, and even though Janice Krochek's directions were still relatively fresh in my mind, I'd gotten lost twice in the maze of Oakland Hills streets and had to stop to consult my map. But all I said to him was, "I'm here now. What's going on?"

"Come on inside. I'll show you."

He led me into the house. Cool in there, almost chilly. And gloomy; there were a lot of arched windows, but all of them were draped in patterned monk's cloth. Tile floors, white stucco walls decorated with Mediterranean-style artwork. I don't know much about art, but the paintings and sculptures seemed original and expensive. Here and there were bare patches where other paintings had once hung. If I'd asked about them, I was pretty sure the answer would be that his wife had sold some of their more valuable pieces to support her habit.

The kitchen was where we went. Big, wide, with a tiled rectangle in the center that held a stovetop, sinks, a dishwasher. The windows here were unshaded, and above the rectangle were a couple of skylights that let in plenty of gray daylight. No sun today, not in the city and not over here.

Krochek stepped around the far side of the rectangle, giving me room to join him. He said, pointing, "There. On the floor."

I went and looked. Hairs stood up on the back of my neck.

Spots and smeared stains, dark and crusty on the light-colored tiles. An uneven trail that led from near the rectangle to an open door at the far end—a laundry room, looked like. I got down on one knee for a closer look at the stains. When I rubbed a finger lightly over one, it came away with a few dry flakes clinging to it. One of the spots was still sticky.

"It's blood, isn't it," Krochek said.

"It's blood. When did you find this?"

"Last night when I got home. I came out here for a drink of water . . ."

"What time?"

"Must've been close to midnight."

"And no sign of your wife?"

"No. I looked everywhere in the house, outside, even in the garage. Her clothes are still in her closet."

"Anything missing out here?"

"Missing?"

"Kitchen utensils. The sharp kind."

". . . Oh. No, the knife rack's full except for the one there by the sink."

I went over and looked. No stains on the shiny blade of the butcher knife on the drainboard. Dirty dishes cluttered the sink, giving off a faintly sour smell.

"I don't suppose you called the police."

"Christ, no," Krochek said. "You know the first thing they'll think, don't you?"

"So you called me instead."

"I didn't know what else to do."

Yeah. "More blood in that room back there?"

"A little, not much."

"Anywhere else in the house?"

"No. Here, just here and the laundry room."

"Anything else out of the ordinary? Signs of disturbance?"

"No. Just the blood."

"You keep a gun in the house?"

"Gun? No. I wouldn't know how to use one."

"Does your wife?"

"No way. She's afraid of guns."

"That's a good thing to be. The laundry room have an outside door?"

He nodded. "It was unlocked."

"You look around outside?"

"Last night and again this morning. Nothing."

"When did you last see your wife?"

"Yesterday morning, before I left for work."

"How did she seem then? Her mood, frame of mind."

"I don't know. She was asleep, or pretended to be."

"How was she the night before?"

"Twitchy and bitchy. Her middle names."

"Did you take her to see a doctor?"

"She wouldn't go. Just kept saying she didn't need one."

"And I don't suppose she gave you any idea of who beat her up?"

"She wouldn't talk about it. Didn't have much to say to me at all. She stayed in one of the guest rooms Monday night, drinking."

"Receive or make any phone calls?"

"Not that I know about," Krochek said. "I checked the answering machine. No messages."

"Did you talk to your neighbors, find out if they know anything?"

"No. I didn't want to talk to anybody until I talked to you. Wouldn't do any good anyway. People mind their own business up here."

"Rebecca Weaver seemed pretty interested on Monday."

"That's because she was out front when you brought Janice home. She's not usually nosy."

"You said you got home around midnight. Why?"

"I don't . . . what do you mean?"

"Why so late? You had a battered wife and an iffy situation here. Where were you?"

Eyeshift. "A business dinner, I couldn't get out of it—"

"Don't lie to me, Mr. Krochek. Not anymore. Not if you want my help."

He gave his lower lip a workout before he said, "All right. I was with a . . . friend."

"What friend? What's her name?"

"Do you have to know that?"

"What's her name?"

"Deanne Goldman. She works for another firm down on the Square. We . . . she has an apartment near Lake Merritt. . . . Look, you have to understand. There's been nothing physical between Janice and me for more than two years. A man has needs, you know how that is . . ."

Justifying himself. His kind of man always does, to others and to himself. I said, "How long has it been going on?"

"A few weeks."

She wouldn't be the first. Nor the last, probably. Janice Krochek, in the Hillman last week: *You think he's some kind of saint? Well, he's not. Far from it.* Some pair. A pair I wished now more than ever that I'd never drawn.

"Will she verify you were with her?"

"Yes, sure, if it comes to that. But I didn't go over to her apartment until after seven."

"No?"

"I worked until five-thirty, had a couple of drinks and a sandwich at the Ladderback."

"Alone?"

"Alone," Krochek said. "I didn't talk to anybody except the waitress and she was busy as hell. Is there any way to tell what time this . . . whatever it was . . . happened? From the blood, I mean."

"Not exactly. Not now."

"You see? If I call the cops, they'll think I came here after work and . . . you know, that I did something to Janice. Because of all the trouble we've been having, the money she's blown. They'll think it was a fight and I killed her. You *know* they will."

"Did you kill her?"

"No!" He looked stricken, as if I'd betrayed him somehow. "I swear to God, I didn't have anything to do with this!"

"Take it easy, hang onto yourself," I said. "Let's go outside—through the laundry room. Watch where you walk—don't step in those blood marks."

He nodded jerkily, led the way into the laundry room. Without touching anything, I looked around in there for signs of disturbance. Nothing. Krochek opened the back door. Tiled patio strewn with outdoor furniture, close-clipped lawn surrounding a kidney-shaped swimming pool with an electric-powered cover drawn over it. Nothing to see on the tiles. On the edge of the lawn near the back-door path there was a short, narrow, crescent-shaped gouge where something heavy had cut into the grass. Not fresh but not too old, either; the mashed-down grass inside the gouge hadn't browned yet. I asked Krochek if it had been there before yesterday.

"I don't remember," he said. "Might've been. Damn gardener gets careless sometimes."

Nothing on the path that led around the side and through a tall locked gate to the driveway. You could get into the garage from the yard; the door there was unlocked. I opened it and looked inside. Empty except for gardening implements and the usual garage clutter. Krochek's Porsche Boxster was parked in the driveway.

We went back into the house. I had Krochek show me the bedroom his wife had occupied Monday night. Rumpled bed, stink of stale cigarette smoke, bottle of Scotch and a smudged glass on the nightstand, the bloodstained clothes she'd been wearing on Monday tossed haphazardly on the floor. Nothing else out of place. Nothing to grab my attention in the adjoining bathroom. We went into his bedroom, the rest of the rooms in the house. Nothing.

The formal living room was the last of them. He flopped into a leather sling chair and massaged his face with the heels of his hands. "Now what?" he said.

"My advice is to call the police. Right now."

"I can't do that. I *can't*."

"It's the right thing, the smart thing."

"No." His head jerked up. "You're not going to call them on your own, are you? Without my consent?"

"Not without more evidence that a crime was committed here."

"That's right," he said, as if another thought had struck him. "That's right. It *could've* been some kind of accident. Janice cut herself with a knife or something. And then called a cab to take her to an ER."

Not too likely, given the blood marks and the way they stopped just short of the laundry room, and the rest of the circumstances. But I said, "It's possible. You could try calling hospitals in the area."

"Yeah. I'm going to clean up those stains, too. I almost did it last night. That's what I should've done."

Instead of waiting to call me, he meant. "I wouldn't advise it," I said.

"Why not?"

"If a crime has been committed here, you'd be guilty of destroying evidence. Police forensics could find traces of blood no matter how many times you scrubbed the kitchen floor."

"There's not that much. It could be anybody's." He massaged his face again. "Christ. You really think she's dead?"

"Do you?"

"I don't know. Maybe. I'm not sure I care if she is . . . no, that's not true, of course I care. I don't know what I'm saying. I just want this nightmare to be over with."

"What is it you want me to do, Mr. Krochek?"

"Find Janice. Find out what happened here."

"I don't know that I can do that. It may not be possible."

"But you can try. You can try."

His eyes pleaded with me. He was close to the edge of panic; you could see it in the twist of his expression, the tautness of his body, the compulsive face-rubbing. I didn't much like the man—weak, selfish people leave me cold—but from his actions and emotional reactions I was pretty sure he wasn't responsible for whatever had gone down here yesterday or last night. And he did seem to have some feelings left for his wife and her safety, despite all she'd put him through. I had sympathy for him, as I did for any poor schmuck who found himself backed into a corner through the actions of others. I could not walk away from him, much as I would have liked to.

"I can try," I said. "On three conditions."

"What conditions?"

"First, that everything you've told me is the truth. If you lied about any of it, if you're withholding anything, I'll find out. And that'll be the end of it."

"I've told you the truth, I swear it. One hundred percent."

"Second condition. You don't clean up any of those bloodstains in the kitchen. Leave them just as they are. Cover them up with something if you can't stand to look at them."

"All right."

"Third condition. Your wife may be dead; we both know that. If I find any conclusive evidence of foul play, or if her body turns up somewhere, I'm obligated to go straight to the police and tell them what I know. I could lose my license if I didn't."

"Where would that leave me?"

"With a choice. Do the right thing and I'll back you up. Otherwise you're on your own."

He agonized over it, but not for long. "Agreed," he said. Then, "So what do we do now?"

"Call the hospitals first. If she's not in any of them, find out if any of your neighbors saw or heard anything and what time. Call me right away if there's anything I should know—I'll give you my cell phone number. After that, stay put for the rest of the day."

"I don't know if I can stand to be cooped up here any longer . . ."

"Force yourself. For all we know, your wife could walk in any minute. If that happens, or you hear from her, or if there are any calls for her, let me know right away."

"What'll you be doing?"

"The best I can," I said, and let it go at that.

Before I left, I let Krochek give me five hundred dollars in cash and had him write me a check for another five hundred. Money isn't everything, but on a lousy case like this, on a lousy hump day, I figured it was a matter of entitlement.

10

The musty furniture in the lobby of the Hillman had one occupant today, an elderly woman knitting what appeared to be a white shawl or afghan with an air of bright-eyed, scowling concentration, like one of the French Revolution ladies waiting for the guillotine blade to lop off another head. The same rusty-haired clerk was behind the desk, playing solitaire with a chewed-up deck. When I got close enough I could see that the backs of the cards were mildly pornographic. He gave me a bored look and made no effort to hide his playthings.

I said, "Ginger Benn. Is she in?"

"Nope."

"Know where I can find her?"

"Nope."

"She works as a waitress. You must have some idea where."

The bored look modulated into one of wariness; he'd recognized me. He quit fiddling with the cards, laid his hands flat on top of them. "You're that cop who was in here last week."

"I'm not a cop."

"No? That's what you said."

"Wrong. That's what you assumed. I'm a private investigator."

"Oh, one of those," he said with a half sneer.

"We were talking about Ginger Benn."

"You were talking about her, not me."

"What's your name?"

". . . My name? What you want to know that for?"

"So I can report you to the management for being uncooperative. Or to the police for withholding information, if it comes to that."

"Hey," he said, "hey."

The knitting woman had been listening; she made a cackling sound. I turned away from the desk and said to her, "Excuse me, ma'am." She looked up from her clicking needles. "What's this man's name?"

The clerk said, "Don't tell him."

The woman said, "*Mister* Phil Partain. He's an asshole."

"Hey," he said again.

"Something wrong with the heat in my room," she said. "That's why I'm down here. *Mister* Partain won't have it fixed."

"Not my problem, Mrs. Grabowski. I told the management about it last week."

"Says he told the management," the woman said to me. "Probably didn't. Doesn't care if old people like me freeze to death."

"Nobody ever froze to death in this hotel."

"Not yet, *Mister* Partain. No thanks to you."

"Old bitch," he muttered under his breath.

Nice place, the Hillman. Homey.

"All right, Phil," I said. "One more time. Ginger Benn."

He hesitated, and I looked hard at him until his eyes shifted. Then he said, "Benjy's Seven. North Beach."

"Topless club?"

"I never been there, I wouldn't know."

"Okay. Now let's talk about Janice Stanley."

"Who?"

"Ginger Benn's roommate. The woman I came here to see last week."

"What about her?"

"Last time you saw her was when?"

"I don't remember. Couple of days ago. Why?"

"Saturday?"

"Might've been."

"Sunday?"

"I don't work Sundays."

"Monday morning?"

"No."

"Was Ginger Benn here Monday morning?"

"They come in, they go out. Half the time I don't even see 'em."

"Ginger say anything to you about her roommate moving out?"

"No. She don't talk to me much."

"So as far as you know, the two of them are still sharing her room."

"Far as I know. Management doesn't care, as long as the tenants pay their rent on time."

"Management doesn't care," Mrs. Grabowski said, "and *you* don't care, either. That's for sure."

Partain said, "What's the idea of all the questions anyhow?"

"You know a man named Carl Lassiter?"

"Who?" His blank look seemed genuine.

"Big, heavyset, well-dressed, tough-looking. He was here to see Janice Stanley right before I came last week."

"I don't remember him."

"You remembered me."

"You were with a black chick and that other guy," Partain said. "That who you mean, the guy you were with?"

"No. Carl Lassiter."

"I see a lot of people and my memory's not so good." He ran the cards together into a stack and began to shuffle them. "You satisfied now?"

The hell with him. We'd rankled each other long enough. I put my back to him and headed out past the knitting woman.

"Told you he was an asshole, didn't I?" she said.

My cell phone rang as I was driving to North Beach. I pulled over into a loading zone before I answered. Tamara. I'd called her on the way back from the East Bay, to fill her in on the situation with the Krocheks and to ask her to do some background checking on Krochek, Deanne Goldman, and Ginger Benn, see what else she could find out about Carl Lassiter.

"First thing," she said. "Remember I told you about the piece of paper I found in Mrs. Krochek's coat? La Farge, s. 1408."

"I remember."

"Well, I'm pretty sure it stands for Hotel La Farge, suite 1408. Number 9 underneath was probably a time—nine p.m., Saturday or Sunday. Could be the guy who beat her up."

"Who occupied that suite on the weekend?"

"Man named Jorge Quilmes. Businessman from Argentina. Big bucks—suites at the La Farge don't go for chump change."

"Find out anything about him?"

"Not much yet. Checking."

"He wouldn't still be registered, would he?"

"As of a few minutes ago. They wouldn't tell me for how long."

"I'll check it out. Anything else?"

"One new thing on Lassiter," she said. "His Caddy is registered to him, but he doesn't own it."

"No? Who does?"

"QCL, Inc."

"Address?"

"That's the interesting part. I can't find an address or phone number, or anything else about them."

"Out of state?"

"Could be. So far it's just a name."

"Okay. Anything on Krochek?"

"Not much. He was married once before."

"Is that right? When?"

"Ninety-four. Mary Ellen Layne. Lasted ten months."

"He file for the divorce?"

"Her. Not the usual irreconcilable differences, either."

"Wouldn't be because of abuse, would it?"

"Uh-uh. Infidelity."

"Krochek contest the settlement terms?"

"Nope. Man didn't have many assets back then. You want me to BG check Mary Ellen Layne?"

"If you have time. What about his girlfriend?"

"Deanne Goldman? Haven't gotten to her yet."

"How about Ginger Benn?"

"Two arrests, one conviction for prostitution. One arrest for possession of a controlled substance—cocaine. No connection with Janice Krochek that I can find so far. How they hooked up, I mean."

I told her where I was headed next. She said, "North Beach strip club, huh? Watch out for those topless dancers."

"I won't even notice."

Tamara laughed. "Yeah, sure. You're not gay and you're not dead. You'll notice, all right."

North Beach has been called the heart and soul of San Francisco. You won't get any argument from me on that assessment. It's one of the city's oldest districts, named for a beach that became landfill in the 1800s, and it has a colorful history and a number of famous landmarks—Russian Hill, Telegraph Hill, Coit Tower, Washington Square, the section of Lombard known as the world's crookedest street. It's old San Francisco and new San Francisco; it's much of the best and some of the worst that the city has to offer. The Barbary Coast was born, grew up wild and corrupt, and died there in the 1906 earthquake. The Beatnik counterculture was founded in North Beach and the neighborhood still retains much of the old Bohemian atmosphere established by Ferlinghetti, Kerouac, and the rest.

For me, it's a place that stirs nostalgic memories. I remember when it was called Little Italy, in those long-ago days when its population was largely made up of Italian immigrants and there were large numbers of Italian social halls and bocce ball courts and opera cafes and family-style restaurants that served the finest meals on the west coast. I remember attending mass with my mother and her relatives at the Saints Peter and Paul Church, and afternoon festivals and picnics in Washington Square. I remember the hungry i, and Enrico's, the city's first outdoor cafe. And I remember the gaudy nightclubs that once lined Broadway—Big Al's, the Roaring Twenties, Finocchio's—and the furor over the topless craze started by Carol Doda at the Condor Club in the early sixties.

Broadway east of Columbus is still the center of adult entertainment, but all the memorable old clubs are gone now and the ones that have replaced them don't have the style or the flare. They're all loud music and blinding neon and aggressive shills and in-your-face sex, with interchangeable names and programs and attitudes. Tourist traps and sleaze palaces, for the most part. Benjy's Seven, just off Montgomery, was one of that breed. I knew it would be even before I tuned out the shill at the door and walked inside.

Dark except for flashing strobe lights, music blaring from hidden speakers, a horseshoe-shaped bar, and seven small, round, raised dancer's platforms spotted at different heights among the tables spread throughout. Benjy's seven. At peak hours, topless dancers would do their thing on the little platforms, wrapping themselves around the brass poles that jutted up phallically from the center of each one. Now only two were in use—one Asian woman, one black woman, both lethargic in their gyrations. There were less than a dozen customers, all male, all grouped around the two dancers, staring with eyes that seemed glazed and zombielike in the swirl of colored light. Places like this, particularly in the afternoon, strike me as bleak and depressing. Men with no lives, no commitments or goals, sucking down cheap liquor while they watched dull-witted women of the same ilk expose their bodies and simulate indifferent sex. It was all about as stimulating and erotic as a visit to a stud farm.

Two scantily clad waitresses worked the tables, neither of them very busy. I went over to the bar, paid too much for a bottle of beer-flavored water, and waited for one of the waitresses to come up to her station. She wasn't Ginger Benn. "You want me to send Ginger over?" she asked. I said yes, and she went away, and pretty soon the other waitress sidled up.

Mid-twenties, blond, busty, big without being fat. Old, cynical eyes sized me up, decided I was nobody she knew, and took on the same blank look as the male customers. Her smile was thin and professional. "I'm Ginger," she said.

"I'm Bill."

"We don't know each other. Somebody give you my name?"

"Not exactly. I'm looking for Janice Stanley."

The smile didn't quite go away. "She doesn't work here."

"I know. But she's a friend of yours."

"Who told you that? I hardly know her."

"Then how come you let her move in with you a month ago?"

Now the smile was gone; the overpainted mouth was drawn tight. "Look, mister, you want to make a date with Janice, go ask somebody else."

"I didn't say I wanted to make a date with her."

"Then what do you want?"

"I told you. I'm trying to find her."

"Why?" Then, warily, "You some kind of cop?"

"A friend of her husband's."

"Yeah, well, I don't know where she is."

"When did you see her last?"

"Few days ago. Friday."

"Heard from her since?"

"No."

"Not even curious why she disappeared all of a sudden?"

"None of my business. I got enough troubles of my own."

"The two of you didn't get along, is that it?"

"We got along. She was just crashing with me for a while, okay? Now why don't you leave me alone, let me do my job?"

"Somebody beat her up on the weekend," I said.

The words stung her enough to make her head jerk, her eyes widen. "Beat her up?"

"That's right. Badly enough to send her back home for a couple of days. Only now she's disappeared again, under suspicious circumstances."

". . . What's that mean, suspicious circumstances?"

"You have any idea who smacked her around?"

"No. How would I know?"

"Or where she might be now?"

"No."

"Friends of hers, people she might go to?"

"We didn't talk much. Didn't see each other much."

"What did she do when she wasn't staying in your apartment?"

Shrug. "Her business, not mine."

"You ever do anything together?"

"Like what? Double dates? No."

"How about gambling?"

"Her thing, not mine. I don't gamble." The shape of her mouth around the word was bitter. "I hate gambling."

"But you took in a compulsive gambler as a roommate."

"I told you—Never mind, forget it. You all done taking up my time now?"

"Not yet." I made a little show of opening my wallet, taking out a twenty, letting her see it before I creased it down the middle lengthwise. "A few more questions."

She licked her lips, her eyes fixed on the creased bill. Waitresses in places like this don't make much money, rely heavily on tips. Call girls don't get to keep a large percentage of their fees, either, unless they run their own service, and Ginger Benn didn't look shrewd enough for that. She wanted that twenty. What she didn't want was to get herself in trouble by talking too much to a stranger.

"I told you, man," she said, "I don't know anything about Janice getting beat up."

"I believe you. But you didn't answer my question about her being your roommate. How'd that come about, if you're not friends?"

"Oh, shit. Okay. A favor, okay?"

"But not to her."

"A friend. A favor for somebody we both know."

"What's the friend's name?"

"Hey, Ginger." That was the bartender; he'd moved down and was leaning across the bar. "Drinks waiting, customers waiting. Shag your ass."

"Yeah, I'm on it." She didn't look at him; her eyes were still coveting the twenty. "Wait here," she said to me. "I'll be right back."

I waited while she put a pair of drinks on her tray, delivered them to one of the tables. The bartender glared at me. So did a young, beefy type with a shaved head at the far end of the bar. Bouncer. I ignored both of them.

Ginger came back with a clutch of bills, handed them over to the bartender. Nobody was allowed to run a tab in a place like this. She hesitated before she came back to where I half-sat on one of the stools. Reluctant, but unable to resist the lure of the twenty dollars.

Her eyes made sure I still had the bill in my hand. Then she moved around so that her back was to the bartender and the bouncer. "You going to give me that? Better do it now if you are."

I dropped it onto her tray. She made it disappear into the shadow between her breasts in a movement as quick and deft as a magician's.

"Okay. But make it quick."

"You were going to tell me the name of the friend of yours and Janice's you did the favor for."

"No, I wasn't. It's none of your business."

"It might be if he knows something about what happened to her."

"What makes you think it was a guy? It wasn't."

A lie. I said, "Carl Lassiter?"

"I don't know any Carl Lassiter." That came out fast—too fast. He was somebody she knew, all right. And the tightening of muscles around her mouth, the flicker of emotion in her eyes, said he was somebody she was afraid of.

"How about a man named Quilmes, Jorge Quilmes?"

"Who?" The puzzlement sounded genuine. "Never heard of him."

"Like you never heard of Carl Lassiter."

"That's right."

"How about QCL, Inc.?"

She couldn't quite stop herself from flinching. QCL, Inc. was something else she was afraid of. "I don't know what you're talking about."

"Sure you do," I said. "Lassiter, Janice, you—all connected to QCL."

"No. You're wrong." Her voice had risen. "Look, why don't you just leave me alone?"

"Let's talk about QCL. I've got another twenty in my wallet—"

"I don't want any more of your money. I don't want any more of *you*!"

Half shriek, that last sentence. As loud as the music was in there, the bartender heard her and hand-signaled the bald-headed guy. The bouncer came our way, not too fast, in a kind of hard glide. At the same time Ginger backed off from me. I took a step toward her, saying, "Wait," but she turned and hurried away into the section where the Asian dancer was simulating sex with the brass pole on her platform. In the next second the bouncer was between us and not quite in my face, like a wall.

"You don't want to bother the girls," he said, low-key.

"I wasn't bothering her. Just a friendly conversation."

"Didn't look so friendly to me. Suppose you have a seat, buy yourself another beer, enjoy the show."

"I've had enough warm beer."

He said, with iron in his voice this time, "Then why don't you go someplace else, pops."

"Yeah, sonny, why don't I." I stayed put, locking gazes with him, just long enough to let him know he wasn't intimidating me, and then took my time walking out of there.

11

The Hotel La Farge, just off Union Square, was one of the city's more venerable hostelries, built in the twenties and renovated at least twice since. Sedate, expensive, respectable. That last, respectable, had a somewhat different meaning these days. Hotels no longer police the morals of their guests, unless something happens that forces the issue. If a guest wants to entertain a member of the opposite sex in his room at any hour, day or night, and the visitor is reasonably presentable, hotel staffs are trained to look the other way. None of their business, and that's as it should be. The worst thing any institution, public or private, can do is to try to dictate morality on any level.

La Farge had an underground garage, valet parking only at a confiscatory fee; I turned my car over to the attendant—another item for the Krochek expense account—and went into the ornate, wood-and-marble lobby. I used one of the lobby phones to call Suite 1408. No answer. At the desk, I asked one of a brace of well-dressed clerks if he knew when Mr. Jorge Quilmes in Suite 1408 would return.

He said, correcting me without making an issue of it, "I believe Señor Quilmes and his party are still in the Blue Room Lounge."

"His party?"

"Two other gentlemen who came to see him a short time ago."

The Blue Room Lounge was a fancy name for a small, not too dark lobby bar. Two couples sat apart from each other at the bar, and three men in business suits were grouped in leather chairs around one of the tables near a gas-log fireplace. It wasn't yet four o'clock, but cocktail hour starts early in the city. I didn't much care for the idea of bracing Jorge Quilmes in company; it looked liked a conference rather than a social situation and people don't take kindly to being interrupted when financial matters are under discussion. But I had a business to run, too, and you do what you need to do when the opportunity presents itself.

The three of them were speaking a mixture of Spanish and English in low tones when I came up. I took the eldest to be Quilmes: mid-fifties, olive-skinned, black hair frosted with gray, mustache and Vandyke beard likewise frosted, dressed expensively and meticulously. The other two were younger, deferential, one of Latino ancestry, the other a blond American with a desultory command of Spanish.

"Excuse me for intruding," I said, "but it's important that I have a few words with Señor Quilmes."

The distinguished type said, "Yes? I am Señor Quilmes," in English with only a trace of accent.

The blond American said, "We're having a business meeting here."

The other Latino said, "Who are you? What is it you want?"

"It's a private matter."

"Can't it wait?"

"I'm afraid not."

"Such an impolite country, America," Quilmes said, but without rancor; almost affectionately, in fact. He even smiled a little, in a tolerant way. "Everything is important, everything must be attended to immediately. What is it you wish to see me about?"

"An appointment you had last Saturday night."

"Appointment?"

"Here at your hotel. At nine o'clock."

Nothing changed in his expression. The other two men looked at him, looked at me, looked at him again. Quilmes and I locked gazes. At least fifteen seconds passed, none of us moving, before Quilmes stirred slightly and said to his companions, "If you will excuse me for a short time. Fresh drinks at the bar, perhaps?"

They didn't argue or waste any time. Both of them got up, the blond brushing past me with a narrow-eyed look, and headed straight across to the bar.

Quilmes said coldly, "You may sit down."

I sat and we looked at each other some more. I put an end to that by producing the photostat of my license and laying the case open flat on the table between us. He leaned forward to study it, leaned back again, and picked up his drink. Still no expression on his aristocratic face.

"Yes?" he said.

"Janice. The woman you had the appointment with Saturday night."

"How do you know I had such an appointment?"

"How I know isn't important. Are you going to deny it?"

Silence. He sipped his drink, set the glass down again, carefully. "In my country," he said at length, "we have laws that carry severe penalities for attempted extortion. You have the same laws, do you not?"

"We do," I said. "And I support them, just as I support ethics in my profession. I'm not here for financial gain or to cause you any undue embarrassment."

"Then why are you here?"

"For the answers to a few questions."

"And if I choose not to answer your questions?"

"That's your prerogative. But it would be in your best interest if you're candid with me. The woman, Janice, has disappeared under . . . let's say unusual circumstances that may involve foul play. If you refuse to talk to me, and her disappearance becomes a police matter, I'd have to tell them about your Saturday-night appointment. And that you were uncooperative when I asked you about it."

He said nothing for maybe thirty seconds. His pupils, in the dim light, were as black as obsidian. Then, "I have a wife and two children in Buenos Aires. I love my family very much. I also have a successful business and many associates, some of whom are quite religious. Do you understand?"

"I understand. If you have nothing to hide and you don't try to stonewall me, there's no reason your name has to be mentioned to anyone. Stonewall means—"

"I know what it means," he said. "Do you think I had something to do with this woman's disappearance?"

"I have no reason to. Information is all I'm after. Provide it, and we'll consider this conversation a private business meeting strictly between the two of us."

I had him and he knew it. "Very well," he said stiffly. "I will answer your questions."

"Good. You did have a date with Janice Saturday night?"

"Yes."

"Here in your suite."

"Yes."

"Had you ever seen her before that night?"

"No."

"How was the date arranged?"

"Through a personal acquaintance."

"His name?"

"I cannot tell you that."

"It wouldn't be Carl Lassiter, would it?"

The slightest hesitation before he said, "I know no one by that name."

"Someone else connected to QCL, Incorporated?"

"Nor any such business."

"How long did Janice stay with you?"

"Not long. One hour, perhaps."

"For which you paid her how much?"

"No money changed hands," Quilmes said.

"No? Who did you pay? The acquaintance who made the arrangement?"

"If you must know, yes."

"Is that always the way it's done?"

"You may think I make a habit of this sort of thing, but I do not. Only once in a great while. A man has needs, and when they become too great to ignore . . . well, we are only human. Surely you understand."

I understood that he was another one like Mitchell Krochek—a self-justifer who relied on the old "a man has needs" wink-wink line when he got caught philandering. Krochek, at least, had some foundation for his affair with Deanne Goldman; Quilmes had none other than pure lust.

I said, "I'm sorry to have to ask this, but it's necessary. What sort of sexual activity was involved?"

Brittle silence. The black pupils had sparklights in them now, like fire opals. He said finally, "I am a man of simple and conventional tastes."

"No sadomasochistic games, then."

"Of course not. I find that sort of thing repugnant."

"Rough sex?"

"That, too."

"So Janice was perfectly healthy when she left you."

"Perfectly. Why do you ask these questions?"

"She was beaten up sometime late Saturday or Sunday. I'm trying to find out who did it and why."

"I see," Quilmes said. He didn't sound sympathetic. "A dangerous profession, prostitution."

"Yes, it is. But Janice isn't strictly a prostitute."

"No?"

"No. Are you a gambling man, Señor Quilmes?"

The question caught him off-stride. He frowned slightly, the first break in his stoic demeanor, before he said, "I do not understand."

"It's a simple question. Do you gamble? Poker, roulette, other games of chance?"

"I fail to see the relevance."

"Please answer the question."

Pretty soon he said, "I fly to San Francisco once a year for business purposes, but not always directly from Buenos Aires. I often spend a few days in Las Vegas."

"The acquaintance who arranged your date with Janice wouldn't happen to be headquartered there, would he?"

"That is of no consequence. I still fail to see how my recreational activities are connected to the disappearance of this young woman."

"Janice is a gambler. A compulsive gambler. That's why she sells her body—to pay for her habit and her debts."

"A pity. But what connection does this have to me?"

"Do you gamble while you're in San Francisco?"

"Seldom," Quilmes said. "Not at all on this visit."

"Do you know any gamblers here?"

Another slight hesitation before he said, "I do not." Territory he didn't want to be breached. He finished his drink, placed his hands flat on the table. The planes of his face had a solidified look, like skin molded too tight over bone. "I did not meet Janice at a gambling establishment. I had never seen her before Saturday night, as I told you. I know nothing of her life or her disappearance. Are you satisfied now?"

"Unless you have anything more to tell me."

He said with a kind of harsh dignity, "I have allowed myself to be stripped naked in front of a stranger. There is nothing more for you to see or know."

"I hope not, Señor Quilmes. Thanks for your time."

The black eyes followed me as I got to my feet, moved away. I could feel them on my back, the cold hate in them, all the way out of the lounge.

It was nearly five by the time I got back to the agency. Tamara was alone in her office, involved with somebody on the phone. I closed the connecting door between our offices, sat down at my desk. Time to check in with Mitchell Krochek.

He must have been draped over his phone; he answered in the middle of the first ring. He sounded less frantic than he had when I'd left him earlier. Booze was the calming influence; he didn't exactly slur his words, but they had a kind of liquidy glide. Yes, he'd followed my instructions, stayed home all day. For nothing. He hadn't heard from Janice or anybody else; no calls, no visitors.

"I talked to some of the neighbors," he said. "Made up a story to explain why I was asking. None of them saw Janice or anybody else around here on Tuesday. I even called her sister in Bakersfield. They're not close, but I thought maybe . . . you know. Ellen hasn't heard from her in months."

"Did your wife ever mention a company called QCL, Incorporated?"

He repeated the name. "I don't think so. No, never heard of it. What kind of company is it?"

"We don't know yet."

"Then why're you asking me about it?"

"Carl Lassiter either works for QCL or owns it." That was as much as I was going to tell him at this juncture. If he needed to know about his wife's prostitution, I'd give him the information when the time came.

"You talk to this man Lassiter?" Krochek asked.

"Not yet."

"Crissake, why not? He must be the one who beat her up—"

"Not necessarily. And he doesn't necessarily have to have anything to do with what happened in your kitchen."

"Who the hell else then?"

"That's what I've been trying to find out," I said. "I've asked you this before, but are you sure you don't know any of her gambling associates? Any local poker club or casino where she was a regular?"

"Positive," Krochek said. "She never talked about it. Hell, I didn't want to know any of those people or places. Why should I? I couldn't make them stop her from throwing my money away."

"Would any of her friends know? The nongambling variety, I mean."

"I doubt it. She cut them off, what few she had, when she caught that goddamn fever of hers."

"Call them, see if they can tell you anything. Anything at all that might help."

"All right."

"One more question. You and your wife made trips to Las Vegas together. Do you know if she went there alone after she got hooked?"

"Yeah. Once, at least, a couple of years ago. Supposed to be visiting an aunt in Seattle for a few days, but she went to Vegas instead. I found the used airline ticket in the trash."

134 • Bill Pronzini

After we rang off, I opened the connecting door and poked my head into Tamara's office. She was off the phone and she had a few things to tell me.

"No QCL, Inc. registered in California," she said. "No address, either, except for Carl Lassiter's on the Cadillac registration. Could be just a dummy name he uses. Or else he's a local rep for an out-of-state company."

"Try Nevada. Las Vegas, specifically."

"Why Las Vegas?"

I told her about my conversation with Quilmes. "He goes to Vegas regularly and I got the impression he knows Lassiter and QCL, Inc. And Janice Krochek spent some time in Vegas."

"Some sort of gambling outfit?"

"Connected to gambling in some way. I'd bet on it."

She laughed. "Dangerously close to a pun there," she said.

"What is? Oh."

"There's another gambling connection, too. Ginger Benn's husband, Jason Benn. Compulsive gambler for years. Owned a big auto body shop, got in so deep he lost it and went bankrupt in ninety-nine."

That explained her bitter hatred of gambling. "You didn't say ex-husband. Still married?"

"Separated."

"How long?"

"Two years. Man ran up a new bunch of debts and she walked."

"Where'd he get the money to keep betting? From Ginger?"

"Could be."

"If she has been supporting his habit, or helping him pay off his debts, or both, it has to be from hooking. She can't make much at that waitressing job of hers."

"Another reason they're separated, maybe."

"Where's he living, did you find out?"

"Daly City," Tamara said. "Works for an auto body shop on San Jose Avenue in the Outer Mission."

I took down both addresses. Could be he knew something about QCL, Inc. that I'd be able to pry out of him. The outfit, whatever it was and whoever was behind it, not only had a gambling connection but judging from what I'd learned from Quilmes, one to prostitution as well. No surprise if it was Vegas-based; the two vices go hand in hand down there. And yet, there was so much of both running wide open in the Nevada desert, there didn't seem to be much need for a shadowy operation like this one seemed to be. More to it than gambling and prostitution, possibly. Drugs, smuggling of goods or humans—all sorts of possibilities.

But the one thing I couldn't figure was how and why this QCL was operating in San Francisco, and apparently in the person of just one man. Carl Lassiter had the answers, but I didn't have enough information or enough leverage to try bracing him. Or, for that matter, enough probable cause that he was responsible for those kitchen blood smears and Janice Krochek's latest disappearance.

12

JAKE RUNYON

The scarf woman's name was Bryn Darby.

He found that out Tuesday night, on his second canvass of the Taraval neighborhood, from a garrulous woman who ran an arts and crafts store near the Parkside branch library. "Oh, yes," she said, "Mrs. Darby. Her first name is Bryn, B-r-y-n, isn't that an odd name? Poor woman. So much tragedy in her life."

"What sort of tragedy?"

"Well, her deformity. And her husband leaving her. She didn't tell me that, but it's what I heard."

"What sort of deformity?"

"Well, I don't know. Something to do with the right side of her face. I've never seen it and she won't talk about it, not that I blame her a bit even if she has become a bit standoffish since it happened."

"When was that?"

"Oh, it must have been about a year ago. Until then she was attractive and very friendly, we had some lovely chats about art. She's an artist, you know. Watercolors and charcoal sketches. I've seen some of them, she's quite talented."

When he got to the apartment he booted up his laptop and ran a quick check on Bryn Darby. Her address was 2511 Moraga Street, just a few blocks away. Age 33. Born Bryn Christine Cordell in Marin County. Married in 1995 to Robert Darby, an attorney with offices on West Portal. Divorce filed by her husband, March of this year. One child, a boy, Robert Jr., age 9. Primary custody granted to the father.

That was as far as he let himself dig. What the hell was he doing, following a crazy compulsion like this? Invading a stranger's privacy, gathering information on her, without any justification. Wrong-headed, unprofessional. Illegal, like the goverment and their covert spying. Like a damn stalker.

Cracking up.

Sometimes, lately, that was just how he felt—as if he were coming apart again, slowly, one little crack at a time, the way he had after Colleen died.

It was Wednesday afternoon before he got back to the Youngblood pro bono case. He preferred to move ahead quickly on his investigations, get them wrapped up ASAP, move on to the next. But other cases, higher-priority cases, kept interfering. One of those, the wrongful death claim for Western Maritime and Life, had taken a couple of new turns that kept him hopping all day Tuesday and Wednesday morning. At least he was busy, a lot of his time accounted for. The busier you were, the less you had to interface with your private demons.

Aaron Myers worked as an office manager for an outfit called Fresh To You Frozen Foods in South San Francisco. Runyon made the mistake of driving down there instead of calling ahead to make sure Myers was on the job today. He wasn't. Out of the office, no reason given. Expected back tomorrow.

He drove back into the city by way of Army Street and stopped at Myers's apartment building in Noe Valley. More wasted time. Nobody answered the bell. He wrote "Call me, please" on the back of one of his business cards and dropped it through the mailbox slot that bore Myers's name.

It was two o'clock when he walked into Bayside Video on Chestnut Street. Youngblood's friend and chess partner, Dré Janssen, was there but busy with a customer. Runyon browsed through the section marked CLASSICS while he waited. *Casablanca,* one of Colleen's favorites. *The Searchers,* one of his in the days when he'd cared about movies as more than just noise producers and time passers. *Young Frankenstein.* Funny film; he remembered Colleen breaking up every time somebody said "Frau Blücher" and horses started whinnying off-camera. It wasn't until after they'd seen it that he found out why the horses kept freaking, that *Blücher* is the German word for glue. Ron had told him—Ron Cain, his former partner, his friend, dead twelve years now in the high-speed chase that had bitched up Runyon's leg and caused him to take an early retirement from the Seattle PD. Colleen, Ron, people he'd cared about—gone. Andrea, too, even though it had been a long time since he'd had any feelings for her. The only family he had left was Joshua, and his son alive was as irretrievably lost to him as all the rest were dead . . .

The customer was leaving now. Runyon went over, introduced himself, and explained why he was there. Janssen's response was a heavy sigh blown through both nostrils. He was tall, thin, freckles like dark spots of rust sprinkled across his cheeks and one of those patches of chin whiskers popular among young men these days. On his lean, ascetic face the whiskers looked like nothing so much as transplanted pubic hair.

"So Brian's in trouble," he said.

"His mother thinks so. So do I."

"Well, I'm not too surprised. But I don't know that I can tell you much—I haven't seen or talked to him in months."

"Mrs. Youngblood told me you and Brian play chess regularly."

"Used to. All in the past now."

"How come?"

"That's the way he wanted it."

"He tell you why?"

"No. You know somebody most of your life, you think you know them pretty well, right? Then all of a sudden something happens to them and they weird out and you realize you didn't know them at all."

"When did Brian start to weird out?"

"More than a year ago."

"In what ways?"

"Well, it started with him not going to church anymore. He used to be real devout—we belong to the same church."

"His mother didn't say anything about that."

"She doesn't know. He told her he was going to a different one, in my neighborhood, but he wasn't. I asked him why and all he'd say was that he had his reasons."

"You think he lost his faith?"

"Must have, somehow. Didn't seem to want anything to do with religion anymore."

"What else happened with him?"

"Well, he started buying things," Janssen said, "expensive computer hardware he didn't really need. High-quality stuff, all the latest advances. Last time I saw him he had four PCs, three laptops, five printers, three twenty-two-inch screens hooked together, modems, motherboards, CD burners, camcorders, all sorts of anti-spy software, you name it."

"How did he explain it to you?"

"He didn't even try. Just said he needed to keep upgrading his system and it wasn't any of my business anyway."

"How else did he change?"

"Distant, withdrawn," Janssen said. "Started holing up in his flat. Wouldn't answer e-mails or acknowledge chess problems I sent him. Wouldn't return phone messages."

"Did you know he was in debt, not paying his bills?"

"Yeah, I heard. I can tell you part of the reason: he lost two of his best consulting jobs."

"How did that happen?"

"He wasn't doing the work. Just didn't seem to care anymore."

"When did this happen?"

"Four or five months ago."

"He tell you this?"

"No. Another friend of his, Aaron Myers."

"Do you know Myers well?"

"Not very. Met him through Brian, but we didn't hit it off. I ran into him later on at a computer trade show at Moscone and we got to talking. He was worried about Brian, too. But neither of us knew what to do about it."

"Might've contacted his mother."

"Myers did that, or started to, but Brian found out and threw a fit, told him to mind his own business. I thought about doing it on my own, but . . . you know, I didn't want to make things worse by sticking my nose in. I figured he'd talk to her on his own if things got bad enough. But he didn't?"

"No. She doesn't know about his weird behavior or financial problems," Runyon said. "All she knows is that somebody beat him up last week."

"Beat him up? Brian?" Janssen looked and sounded amazed. "Who?"

"He told his mother he was mugged. He told me he was carjacked."

"And you don't believe it's either one."

"Can you think of another explanation?"

"No. Brian's totally nonviolent. If you've met him . . ."

"Monday afternoon, at his flat. His girlfriend was there with him."

"Girlfriend?"

"Brandy. You know her?"

"No way. I never met anyone named Brandy."

Runyon described her and her foul mouth, summarized the scene at Youngblood's flat.

"That doesn't make any sense," Janssen said. "I can't imagine Brian letting *anybody* talk that way about his mother. He didn't stand up to this Brandy at all?"

"Not for a second."

"Man. She sounds like a . . . whore."

"I wouldn't be surprised."

"Brian and a woman like that?" Head wag. "That's just crazy."

"Not the type he's attracted to?"

"Lord, no. His mother tell you he was engaged to Ginny Lawson?"

"Yes."

"You talked to her yet? Ginny?"

"Not yet."

"When you do you'll see what I mean. She's the total opposite of this Brandy—*total*. Real devout. Her hobby is singing gospel music."

"Why did she break off the engagement, do you know?"

"Brian wouldn't say. I figured it must have something to do with the weird way he was acting."

"So it wasn't the breakup that led to his erratic behavior."

"No. The weird stuff started a few months before."

"And for no apparent reason that you could see."

"None. Just . . . out of the blue, seemed to me."

"Has Brian dated any other women since Ginny Lawson?"

"Besides this Brandy? Not that I know of."

"Before Ginny?"

"Well, Verna Washington. She was kind of funky."

"Funky how?"

"Oh, the way she dressed, her tastes in music and food. She's a chef for some restaurant in SoMa. They seemed like kind of an odd couple, but she wasn't nasty or anything."

"How long were they together?"

"Not long. Couple of months."

"What broke them up?"

"Don't know. You'd have to ask him. Or Verna."

"You have an address for her?"

"She was living in the outer Sunset back then. Lake Street, I think. I don't know the number."

Easy enough to find out. Runyon made a note. Then he asked, "Did you know Brian paid off most of his debts three months ago—ten thousand dollars' worth?"

Janssen showed surprise again. "No, I didn't know. Where'd he get that kind of money?"

"I was about to ask you the same question. Certificate of deposit or IRAs, possibly?"

"No way. His family never had much and he's never been big on future planning. He and Ginny argued about it once that I know about."

"Loan from a friend? Aaron Myers?"

"Not Myers—he doesn't have that kind of money. And if Brian has any other friends with that much cash to loan out, I don't know who they could be. Maybe he got it from a bank or finance company."

"He didn't." It would have been on the credit report if he had. "How about new consulting work?"

"That's out, too. Even if he hustled two or three new

jobs, it'd've taken him a lot longer than a month or two to raise that much cash."

Which left what? A couple of possibilities, one of them—

"Brandy," Janssen said abruptly, as if reading his mind. "Maybe *she* loaned it to him. It'd explain why he let her talk smack about his mother, wouldn't it? Why he let her walk all over him?"

"It might."

Janssen shook his head again. "I just don't understand it," he said. "How does a guy like Brian, a good guy, all of a sudden get so screwed up?"

Runyon said nothing. The woman in the scarf, Bryn Darby, flicked across his mind. Most of us can't even explain to ourselves why we screw up or get screwed up in all the ways we do.

He was starting to forget what Colleen looked like.

Always before he could close his eyes and she would appear bright and crystal sharp in his memory. Happy, sad, playful, serious, loving—all her moods, all her voices distinct down to the finest nuance, as if she were still alive and caught by time. She was still there for him now, but the images had begun to blur and fade at the edges. It happened all of a sudden, it seemed to him, like home movies shot with an old video cam that he'd watched one too many times. More and more, now, he found himself looking at his photos of her, the one in his wallet and the framed portrait he kept on the bedside table, to try to recapture the clarity. But it wasn't working. Photos were static, without the movement, the words, the life force—the real Colleen—that had once dominated his memory.

It happened again that night in the apartment. He was in the kitchen making tea, he thought of her, he closed his eyes, and her face came to him in soft focus, as if he was looking at her through a thin mist. He went into the bedroom, sat on the bed, and stared at the framed photograph. Impulse drove him to the closet, where he kept the albums she'd put together before the cancer was diagnosed—snapshots taken at mountains, lakes, Seattle locations, Whidbey Island, Mount Rainier, Vancouver, Victoria Island. He sat with one of them open on his lap and paged through it slowly, looking only at those of her alone or the two of them together with her the most prominent figure. He went all the way through the album before he closed his eyes and looked at the memory images again.

Still the soft, misty focus. Blurred. Faded.

It scared him. He felt as if he were losing her all over again. First Colleen herself, now his memories of her. One day he might close his eyes and not be able to see or remember her clearly at all. If that happened, he didn't know what he would do. He didn't want to think about what he might do.

He put the album away, went into the front room, and turned on the TV. He was sitting there, staring at faceless people talking in a room, when his cell phone rang. The noise activated him again. Business—Bill or Tamara. An emergency, maybe, something to occupy his mind and his time, help him make it through another night.

But it wasn't Bill or Tamara. A half-muffled man's voice

said, "Jake Runyon?" He acknowledged it, and the voice said, "If you want to know who hurt Brian Youngblood and why, ask Nick Kinsella. Nick Kinsella, Blacklight Tavern." That was all. The line went dead.

Runyon switched off. No emergency, but at least now he had something else to think about. The muffling had been the result of a handkerchief or some other cloth draped over the mouthpiece, but it hadn't done much of a job of disguising the voice. Enough of the thin, pale tone had come through to make it recognizable.

Brian Youngblood.

And why would Brian Youngblood want to tell him something anonymously that he could have volunteered straight out, over the phone or in person?

13

TAMARA

She spent Wednesday night with her folks in Redwood City, part of it in a big argument with Pop. Nothing new in that; seemed like she'd spent most of her life facing off with him about one thing or another. She loved him, he loved her, but they were oil and water when they were together and always had been. That was why she'd been such a stone bitch rebel as a teenager, defying Pop and jerking his chain every chance she had. Sex, drugs, and rock and roll drove him crazy, the main reason she'd been such a wild child on all three fronts.

What it boiled down to was, he resented her independence and she resented his need to control everybody and everything—her, Ma, Claudia, the Redwood City police department, the damn gophers and crab grass in his backyard. And when you threw in what Bill called the generation gap, you had a recipe for friction just about every time they saw each other. Big day if they agreed on *anything*. If she said the earth revolved around the sun, he'd find some way to argue the point and twist things around so she was wrong and he was right.

She knew going in that he'd probably be against what she was of a mind to do, but she figured she might as well give it a shot. Thing was, and she'd only admitted this to herself a couple of years ago, she'd always craved the approval, at least some of it, that he gave kiss-ass Claudia in pretty much everything *she* did. Closest he'd come to spooning some out to her was telling her he thought she'd done "a good job" with the agency, but then he'd had to go and spoil it by lecturing her on the dangers of detective work and offering a lot of unwanted advice. He'd tossed a hissy fit when he found out about the day last Christmas—the day the whack job with the load of guns invaded the old agency offices and held her and Bill and Jake hostage for a few hours. Another fit in March, when she'd been kidnapped by that child-stealing son of a bitch in the East Bay. Actually tried to talk her into giving up the partnership after that episode—for her own safety, he said.

Well, the threat of danger was what she wanted to talk to him about now. Strictly business, very professional. Her taking control of the situation, right? That's the way she looked at it. Plus it was an offer of some father-daughter bonding. He couldn't object to that, could he? Naïve, girl. Like hell he couldn't.

So she called up Ma and asked her if Pop would be home tonight, and she said he would, he was working the day shift this week. Ma was always glad to hear from her, always glad to invite her for dinner; they had a pretty good relationship now, at least. Stage set, everything cool.

And everything stayed cool through one of Ma's famous braised short-ribs meals. They all had a glass of wine—just one glass, all Pop allowed except on holidays and then, wow, you could actually have two glasses as long as you put plenty of space between the first and the second—and he seemed to be in a pretty good mood. He'd helped catch a serial rapist and he did a little justifiable bragging about it, which was rare because he usually didn't like business rap at the dinner table. Afterward she said she'd had a little business matter to talk over with him, and they went into his den and sat down.

He looked good, she thought. Buff, even, not a hint of flab anywhere. She felt a stab of jealousy. Must be nice not to ever have to worry about your weight. His hairline had receded about halfway back on his knobby head, the reason he wore his "lucky Fedora," a shapeless gray hat with a moldy bird feather in it, everywhere except in the house; he'd probably be bald as an egg in another few years. That was something she'd never have to put up with, anyway.

"Talk to me, sweetness," he said.

Sweetness. She didn't much like that nickname; sometimes, when he pissed her off enough, she actively hated it. "I've been thinking," she said, "it's about time I got myself firearms certified."

He'd been favoring her with his fatherly smile. Amazing how quick it could turn into his stern, disapproving fatherly scowl. He said, "What brought that on?" and his tone had dropped to one decibel above a growl.

What had brought it on was the happenings last Christmas and March, and what had brought it to the point where she was ready to do something about it was Janice Krochek walking into the office unannounced and all beat up on Monday morning. Nothing really ominous in that, but what if the dude who'd done it had followed her in and started more trouble? What if something like the Christmas invasion or the kidnapping happened again? It could. Bad things happened in threes, right? She didn't want to get into explanations with Pop, but avoiding them with Sergeant Dennis Corbin, Redwood City PD's hotshot interrogator, was next to impossible. Should've remembered that, too.

"Something else has happened," he said before she could open her mouth. "What this time?"

"Nothing's happened, Pop."

"Then how come the sudden urge for firearms certification?"

"Something I've been thinking I ought to do, that's all."

"Why?"

"For protection. Always telling me I need to be more careful, right?"

"Guns aren't toys, Tamara."

"Don't I know it? I've had enough of 'em shoved in my face this year."

His lips thinned down, the way they always did when he was annoyed and trying to hang onto his temper. "And now you want to start shoving one of your own in somebody else's face."

"That what you think I am? Some damn cowboy?"

"Don't use that snotty tone with me. You know I don't like it."

Here we go again, she thought. "Listen, Pop," she said, trying to keep a hitch on her own temper, "I'm not always going to be chained to a desk. I'd like to get out into the field once in a while—"

"Out into the field. Christ."

"Well, why not?"

"You're forgetting what happened the last time you tried to conduct a simple stakeout."

"All right, so I screwed up. Big fucking deal. I won't—"

"Don't use that kind of language in this house."

"Okay, sorry, but you're getting me all worked up."

"I'm your father. Show a little respect."

Show *me* a little respect and I will. But she didn't say it. She said through clamped teeth, "I made a mistake. Everybody makes mistakes."

"A mistake that almost got you killed."

"A mistake that saved a little girl's life."

He had no comeback for that, just sat there and glowered.

"Point is," she said, "I won't make that kind of mistake again. But things happen in my business same as yours, things you can't always be on guard against. Makes sense to be prepared."

"And you just decided this without any provocation."

"Not exactly. Been thinking on it for a while now and it's time."

"Have you talked to Bill about this?"

She'd intended to today, but he'd come into the office with a grouch on and when he was in that kind of mood he was as stubborn as Pop. Catch him at the right time, he'd agree that it made good sense and wouldn't try to talk her out of it.

"Not yet," she said.

"He won't like it any more than I do."

She didn't argue with him. Only make this harder going than it already was.

"You've never fired a gun in your life," he said.

"First time for everything."

"Not everybody's made for it. Some people can't get the hang, can't shoot straight when they do. People who aren't comfortable and accurate with handguns shouldn't keep them around."

"I thought maybe you could teach me," she said. "At the police firing range."

He was mum on that.

"I'd like it if you would, Pop. Be a way for the two of us to spend some time together . . ."

"Firing handguns isn't my idea of quality time."

"Family that shoots together stays together."

"That's not funny," he said, tight-assed again. "I suppose you want me to help you pick out a weapon, too."

"Once I have my permit."

"Carry permit? Is that what you're after? Walk around with a piece stuffed into your purse?"

"No. Keep it at the office, or in the car if I'm working field."

"Lord," he said. He popped a stick of spearmint gum into his mouth and chewed the hell out of it. What he really wanted was a cigar, but his doctor had made him give them up a couple of years ago. "Guns, detective work. You know I never wanted you or your sister to get into law enforcement."

"You only told me about three million times."

He gave her the old half-glum, half-evil-eye parent look. "That sassy mouth of yours'll get you in some big trouble one of these days."

She'd heard that about three million times, too. She forced a smile and shrugged and said, "So how about it, Pop? Us going to the range together, you teaching me."

"I don't think so. It's not a good idea."

"Why not?"

"I don't think you're the type who should be firearms qualified."

". . . What's that mean?"

"Just what I said. You and guns . . . no, I don't like it."

"What don't you like?"

He worked on the gum some more. Made her itch when he did that; people who chewed gum like cows chewing their cuds were bad enough, but the hard, juicy chompers like Pop gave her fits. "I just don't think you're the right fit," he said.

"No, huh? What's the right fit, Pop? Cops, muggers, and NRA cold-dead-handers?"

"Most NRA members are responsible gun owners."

"Since when do you have to be a gun nut to be a responsible gun owner?"

"Don't start in with that liberal crap—"

"Yeah, right. Charlton Heston in black face."

"You better watch it, girl."

"Or what, Pop? You'll paddle my behind?"

"Same old smartass anger. When're you going to learn to control yourself?"

"When you stop putting me down every time we talk."

"I don't put you down—"

"The hell you don't!"

"Keep your voice down, Tamara."

Now he'd really pissed her off. "That's your answer to everything, isn't it? Throw out orders, treat me like a damn kid. Well, I'm not a kid anymore. And I'm not a wild teenager or a militant college student, I'm a grown woman running a business and doing a job that's not much different than yours. You treat your cop buddies with respect, why can't you do the same for your own daughter!"

He glared at her. She glared back.

Knock on the door and Ma came in. "What's all the yelling in here?"

Pop snapped, "Ask her."

She said, "Ask him."

"Well?"

"She's decided she wants to buy herself a handgun," he said. "Start carrying one around in her car."

"For protection, in case of emergencies," she said. "I wanted Pop to teach me to shoot, help me get qualified, but I guess it's just too much to ask."

Ma looked at her, at Pop, back at her again. One of those long, steady looks she always used when she had to step in between them. Ma, the mediator, the voice of reason. "Well," she said finally, "I think it's a good idea."

Surprised her a little, and drove Pop up out of his chair, clouds all over his big face. "You what?"

"You heard me, Dennis. Her work can be as dangerous as yours—you know as well as I do how close we came to losing her twice this year. She has as much right as you to own a gun, learn how to protect herself."

"She's too young, too inexperienced . . ."

"Too flakey, he means," Tamara said.

"I never said that."

"Didn't have to."

"All right, that's enough," Ma said. She went over to him, got up in his face. Little woman, Ma, but she could be tough as hell when she needed to be. "Tamara's as stubborn as you are when her mind's made up. If this is what she wants, then she's going to have it no matter what you say. You want some stranger to teach her about guns instead of her own father? You should be proud she came to you, not getting into an argument you can't win."

He couldn't win an argument with Ma, either. She knew how to handle him, the right buttons to push. Took a little time but the clouds started to break up. He said reluctantly, "Maybe you're right."

"Damn straight," she said. "Tamara, apologize to your father for yelling at him."

She did it; she wasn't pissed anymore, either.

"Your turn, Dennis."

He couldn't do it. Not in so many words. That was Pop for you—hard, inflexible, strictly old-school macho. But it was all right because what he said was, "I'm free Saturday afternoon. I suppose we could go out to the police range then."

Tamara said, "How about one o'clock?"

"One o'clock. All right."

Damn if she didn't feel a moment of tenderness toward both her parents. She grinned across at them.

"Well, that was easy," she said.

Pop's mouth twitched, twitched some more, and he burst out laughing.

Well, what do you know, she thought, grinning. She'd not only made him laugh, which was rare enough in their relationship, but for once she'd also had the last word.

14

My mood on Thursday morning was considerably better than it had been on Wednesday, but Tamara's was downright ebullient. All smiley-faced and energetic. I thought maybe she'd finally met somebody new, after the months of monastic living, but no, that wasn't it.

"Made up my mind to get firearms certified," she said. "Going out to the pistol range with Pop on Saturday for the first lesson."

It took me a few seconds to digest that, and then all I could think of to say was, "Well."

"Not against it, are you?"

Five years ago, given her immaturity, I would've been. Two years ago I'd have tried to argue her out of it. Now . . .

"No, I'm not against it. It's probably a good idea. And your dad'll be a good teacher."

"I thought so, too. Not that you or Jake wouldn't have been as good . . ."

"I'm a little rusty and I don't think Jake practices as often as he should, either. No, you made the right choice."

"Now all I have to do is convince Pop of it."

I went in to check my voice mail messages. Among them was a brief one from Mitchell Krochek. He had no news; he wanted to know if I had any. The callback number he left was his cellular.

"Janice isn't in any of the East Bay or San Francisco hospitals," he said when I got him on the line. "I called them all. Her friends, too . . . the women who used to be her friends. None of them has heard from her in over a year. I was hoping maybe you . . ." He let the rest of it trail off.

"Not yet. You'll hear from me if I have anything to report."

"I don't know how much more of this I can take," he said. "I didn't sleep last night. If I don't hear something by five o'clock, I'll go home and see what's what but I'm not staying there alone again tonight. I'll be at Deanne's."

Deanne Goldman, the girlfriend. "What's her number and address?"

He gave them to me. She lived in Oakland, near Lake Merritt.

After we rang off I spent a little time going over the file on Janice Krochek. Tamara had put it together when we were first hired to track her down and I thought there might be something in it that would give me a lead.

Born in Bakersfield, where her sister Ellen still lived. Parents divorced, father deceased five years ago, mother remarried and living in Florida. Moved to the Bay Area in 1996 to attend UC Berkeley. Majored in business administration, one of those catch-all degree pursuits that young people take when they have no set goals or special interests or skills. Left school after two and a half years—deteriorating grades, poor study habits. Her computer abilities were good enough to buy her a job as a "systems trainee"—glorified name for clerk-typist—at Five States Engineering, where she'd met Mitchell Krochek; they were married less than a year later. Pregnant the second year they were together, terminated by abortion. The pregnancy was an accident, according to Krochek; neither of them wanted children. By his lights, the marriage had been "pretty stable" until her gambling mania began to spiral out of control.

The Krocheks had a circle of friends, but they were what he called "couples friends"—other married people they saw in pairs and groups. Janice Krochek had no close women friends. She'd been something of a loner her entire life, kept things about herself private even after the marriage; he confessed that he'd thought he knew her well but now was sure he never really had. Her big passion as a teenager had been video games—no surprise, since a compulsive gambling addiction often starts with that sort of dissociative activity. It also explained her preference for Internet betting.

No police record or brushes with the law. No extramarital affairs; Krochek was positive of that, though his certainty might have been more ego than actual knowledge. No jobs after the marriage, nor any volunteer work or other outside activities. No hobbies or interests other than computers and gambling. Your typical bored wife of a well-to-do professional husband who had too few friends and interests, too much time on her hands, and carte blanche with his income.

Nothing, no potential lead, in any of that.

Tamara was on the QCL hunt; with any luck she'd turn up something in the next hour or so. Meanwhile, I had some other work to finish up. Routine business that didn't completely engage my attention. The door between my office and the outer office was open; I heard Jake Runyon come in and exchange a greeting with Alex Chavez, who was pecking out a report on his laptop at one of the desks. I also heard what Runyon said next.

"Question, Alex. You know a man named Kinsella, Nick Kinsella?"

"Heard the name somewhere. Give me a second . . ."

I got up and went out there. "What about Nick Kinsella, Jake?"

"Know him?"

"Oh, yeah, I know him. Loan shark. One of the slickest in the city."

"Sure," Chavez said, "now I remember. Rough trade."

"Very. Operates out of a place called the Blacklight Tavern, on San Bruno Avenue west of Candlestick. Charges a heavy weekly vig. Miss a payment or two, get a visit from his enforcers."

Runyon said, "Sounds like you'd have to be pretty desperate for money to go to him."

"Desperate, foolish, and naïve."

"That's Brian Youngblood in a nutshell."

"The pro bono case?"

He nodded. "I had a call last night. If it's legit, Youngblood borrowed ten thousand dollars from Kinsella to pay off his debts."

Briefly he laid out the situation with Brian Youngblood. I listened, but a part of my mind had slipped back to the Krochek case. Nick Kinsella. Loan shark. If QCL, Inc. and Carl Lassiter were in the same business, Kinsella might well know about it. And if he didn't, he'd sure as hell want to. The one thing sharks hate more than anything except dead-beat customers is competition for their blood money.

Chavez said when Runyon was finished, "Funny Young-blood would call you anonymously like that. Why not just identify himself?"

"Yeah. Unless it's got something to do with the girl-friend, Brandy. He's afraid of her."

"He's got worse people to be afraid of," I said, "if he's into Kinsella for ten grand and missing payments. A cracked rib and a few bruises is just warm-up stuff for that bastard's enforcers."

"How approachable is Kinsella?" Runyon asked. "Think I could get him to talk to me about Youngblood?"

"No, but maybe I can." And I told him why. Some time back I had tracked down a bail jumper for a bondsman I did business with now and then, Abe Melikian. The jumper was somebody Kinsella had a grudge against. He liked me for helping put the man in San Quentin, enough to favor me with some information on a couple of other cases. It had been a while since our paths last crossed, but he might be willing to talk to me again, give me some straight an-swers. Particularly if it turned out there was something in it for him.

I went back into my office and called Kinsella's private number at the Blacklight. Somebody who didn't give his name answered, said that Mr. Kinsella wouldn't be in until later. I gave him my name and asked for a callback, ASAP. A small favor, I said, that might turn out to be mutual. I don't like dealing with human parasites like Kinsella; if it were up to me, the fat son of a bitch would be occupying a prison cell with the bail jumper. But sometimes you have to wallow in the gutters they live and work in to get what you need for the greater good. Detective work is a little like modern politics in that respect.

Tamara came into my office a short time later, while I was wrapping up a report on a routine skip-trace. Runyon and Chavez had both gone and I still hadn't heard back from Kinsella.

"QCL, Incorporated," she said. "Las Vegas, sure enough. QCL stands for Quick Cash Loans."

"Surface-swimming sharks."

"Yeah, and their meat is the gambling industry. From all I can find, they specialize in loans to gamblers."

"The steady-loser type. Problem gamblers who can't get a loan anywhere else."

"Right. At humongous interest rates."

"Who runs it?"

"Listed CEO is a dude named Adam O'Dell. Nothing on him yet."

"Carl Lassiter?"

"On the Board of Directors, along with five others—none

of 'em with Vegas addresses. San Francisco, L.A., San Diego, Phoenix, Seattle, Denver."

"So that's the way they work it," I said. "Not too hard to figure the prostitution angle now. Loan cash to compulsives like Janice Krochek, and when they can't pay off on their own, force them into prostitution to do it."

"And if they're men—their wives and girlfriends."

"Yeah. Coercion or threat of bodily harm."

"Ginger Benn?"

"Could be. The johns, most of them anyway, are high rollers who visit Vegas regularly and live or have business interests in the cities you named. Men like Jorge Quilmes."

"Some sweet little racket," Tamara said.

"Some vicious racket, and not so little. Question is, how violent are QCL's methods? How far will they go when somebody balks or steps out of line?"

"Carl Lassiter can answer that."

"So can somebody else, maybe. Ginger's husband, Jason Benn."

15

The auto body shop where Jason Benn worked was on San Jose Avenue near where it intersects with Mission Street. Outer Mission District, the neighborhood where I'd been born and raised. The big, rambling house I grew up in had been only a few blocks away, in what in those days was a little Italian working-class enclave. Gone now, the enclave and the house and the big walnut tree in the backyard where I spent a lot of solitary afternoons, everything torn down and ripped up to make way for a cheaply built apartment complex that was already going to seed.

I don't feel nostalgia when I come out here, as I do when I visit North Beach. Too many sad, painful memories overshadowing the good ones of my mother, a big, sweet-faced woman who had borne heavy crosses with a cheerful smile and heart full of love. Ma. Close my eyes and I can still see her in the kitchen, the one room in the house that was completely hers, making focaccia alla salvia, torta pasqualina, trippa con il sugo di tucco—all the other Ligurian dishes from her native Genoa. I can still smell the mingled aromas—garlic, spices, simmering sauces, frying meats, baking breads and cakes and gnocchi. Good memories, those, savored memories, but the rest . . . no.

My old man is one among the rest. My sister Nina, dead of rheumatic fever not long after her fifth birthday, is another. Black hair, black eyes, so thin her arms and legs were like bare olive sticks—that's all I can remember of Nina. I can't dredge up the slightest image of what my father looked like, but I remember him, all right, the son of a bitch. He was a drunk. Tolerable when he was sober, if a little cold and distant, but grappa and wine and whiskey turned him into an abusive terror. He drank most of the time when he wasn't working, and when he wasn't working was most of the time. He lost one longshoreman's job after another until nobody would hire him anymore, not even relatives. His other vice was gambling—lowball poker and the horses—though it never reached the destructively addictive stage of pathologicals like Janice Krochek. From the time I was old enough to understand about money, I wondered where he got enough every week to pay the bills and feed his habits. It wasn't until the year before I graduated from high school that I found out he was mixed up in a black-market operation on the Embarcadero.

The liquor destroyed his liver, finally put him in the hospital, and killed him within a week of his admission. Ma stood by him to the end, in spite of the abuse. But it took a deadly toll on her. The more he drank, the more she ate for solace and escape; she weighed nearly 250 pounds when she died, too young, at the age of fifty-seven. I hated him for what he did to her. But his selfish, uncaring, drunken ways did me one favor; they helped shape the man I grew into. I don't drink hard liquor and I don't steal and cheat and I don't hurt the people close to me. In all the ways that count, I'm not my old man's son.

No, I don't feel nostalgia when I come back to the old neighborhood. It was all such a long, long time ago, yet the memories still have the capacity to hurt and to bring the sadness flooding back . . .

Crouch's Auto Body was housed in an old, rundown, grimy-fronted building flanked on one side by an industrial valve company and on the other by a fenced-in automotive graveyard piled high with unburied metal corpses, their skeletal bodies and entrails plundered by the Crouch ghouls. Waves of noise—hammers, mallets, hissing torches, power tools—rolled out at me from the droplit interior. Smells, too, dominated by petroleum products and hot metal. Three men were working in there, one with an acetylyne torch on the battered front end of a jacked-up SUV. The first one I approached directed me to the man with the torch. I stood by, watching Jason Benn work, waiting until he was done before I approached him.

He was weightlifter big, heavy through the shoulders but going soft in the middle. Tattoos curled up both forearms; another, some sort of sun symbol, was visible between the collar of his workshirt and black hair long enough for a ponytail. From all of that I expected a loutish face and dim little eyes, but when he finally shut down the torch and took off his protective goggle mask, I was looking at plain, heavy, but alert features and the dark eyes of a man who has lived through his share of hell.

He didn't react when I told him who I was, showed him the photostat of my license, or when I said, "I'm investigating the disappearance of a woman who goes by the name of Janice Stanley."

"What's that have to do with me?" Not hostile, just mildly curious. "I never heard of her."

"She was your wife's roommate for the past month."

"Yeah? I still never heard of her."

"You and your wife don't talk much, I take it."

"Not much. We're separated."

"So I understand. I had a talk with her yesterday."

"And she sent you to me?"

"No. She didn't mention you."

"Then what makes you think I know anything about this missing woman?"

"Janice Stanley has a gambling problem," I said. "The serious kind."

His eyes narrowed. He didn't say anything.

"And she's involved with a man named Lassiter, Carl Lassiter, and a Las Vegas outfit called QCL, Inc."

Long, steady stare. His face grew hard; you could see it happening, like time-lapse photography run at maximum speed. One of the other workmen fired up an electric sander, set it screaming against the Bondoed door of a crash victim. Benn frowned at the sudden noise, stepped toward me, and mouthed the words, "Let's take a walk."

We went through the garage, out a side door into the automotive graveyard. Cracked asphalt with weeds growing up through it; nobody around, just cars passing on the street beyond the fence. Pale sun rays filtering down through a milky overcast gleamed off the surfaces of the decaying corpses, struck micalike glints from broken glass and patches of rust. Benn shut the door to cut off the interior noise, turned to face me.

"Okay," he said. "What do you know about Lassiter and QCL?"

"QCL stands for Quick Cash Loans. Moneylenders to addicted gamblers at high interest rates. Lassiter's their San Francisco agent."

"That all?"

"No. They've got a sideline. Prostitution, the call-girl variety."

"Goddamn it," he said, but the heat in the words was not directed at me. "She tell you all that? Ginger?"

"No."

"Then how'd you find it out?"

"I'm in the detective business. Finding out things is what I do."

Benn half-turned away from me, turned back again, and slapped one fisted hand into the palm of the other. But it wasn't an aggressive gesture. Frustration mixed with anger.

"She's hooking again, isn't she?" he said.

"I don't know."

"Don't bullshit me, man."

"Straight answer: I don't know."

"Sure she is. This woman you're looking for, you say she's got the fever and Ginger took her in. She wouldn't do that if she wasn't hooking for QCL again."

"Why would she start hooking again?"

Smack. Smack. "She promised me, she swore she wouldn't let them pressure her anymore." Smack. "Goddamn it. I make enough now, I'm handling the payments. What the hell's the matter with her?"

"How much do you owe them?"

"Never mind how much, that's my lookout. I'm clean now, I'm dealing with it. She don't have to do that shit anymore."

"Maybe she isn't. You don't know that she is."

"You don't know she isn't. I don't know. She wouldn't tell me the truth if I beat the crap out of her."

"Is that how you got her to promise to quit?"

"What?"

"By beating the crap out of her."

"No. Hell, no. You think I'm that kind? Well, you're wrong, buddy. I said 'if.' I wouldn't hurt Ginger, never. I love her, she loves me."

"Then why'd she walk out on you?"

"She didn't walk out, we made a deal. Live apart for a while, I stay clean and make the payments regular, she quits hooking for those bastards."

"Her apartment at the Hillman," I said. "Who pays the rent?"

"She does. What, you think QCL set her up?"

"Isn't that how they operate?"

"No. All they do is arrange dates and take the money, every fuckin' dime."

"Lassiter, you mean."

"Yeah, Lassiter. I told her stay away from him, I begged

her, why didn't she listen to me." Smack. "I ought to pay him a visit. Bust him in half, the son of a bitch. But then where I'd be? Still up shit creek, that's where."

"What would Lassiter do if one of the women couldn't make the loan payments and refused to go out on any more dates?"

"Do?"

"Slap her around? Beat her up?"

"Not him, not that bastard. He don't operate that way. QCL don't operate that way."

"You sure about that?"

"Sure I'm sure. They're too smart for that."

"Somebody beat up the woman I'm looking for," I said. "I thought it might be Lassiter."

"He wouldn't dirty his hands. Not him. Mr. Cool. Mr. Clean, all dressed up in his expensive suits."

"Nonviolent."

"Yeah." Smack. "He ever touched Ginger, I'd've killed him. He knows it, too. He don't want a piece of me."

"So how do he and QCL operate?"

"Pressure, that's how. Oh, yeah, they know how to put the pressure on once they got their hooks in you. You don't make your payments, they dangle more cash, give you betting tips, set you up in a game somewhere, get you thinking maybe you'll hit a lucky streak—drive you right back down again. Then you got no choice. You work for them one way or another."

The subtle, insidious kind of pressure. No need to use force. The addiction was enough, the offer of a fast loan and the lure of a quick score that would pay off the debts and put the addict back in the driver's seat. Most of the time the losers lost and the hook got set even deeper. If one of them won once in a while, that'd be okay with QCL. Same principle the casinos operated on; good business when somebody beat the house because it tantalized the losers, made them bet more and more trying to be the next winner.

"Not me, not anymore," Benn said. "They can't drive me back into the gutter. I'm clean, I'm making my payments right on time. They got no more leverage with Ginger. Unless . . . She didn't lose her job, did she? That lousy T & A club where she works?"

"No."

"Then she's got no reason to start hooking again. She hated doing it—hated it. Did it for me, that's how much she loves me. And I let her. Shitheel Jason *let* her."

"I don't think she's hooking anymore, Benn."

"No? You said you didn't know."

"I don't. Just a feeling I have after talking to her."

"Then why'd she let this woman, this gambling junkie, move in with her?"

"Pressure," I said. "Just a little. Keep her in line in case you backslide."

"Yeah. Yeah, that'd be just like Lassiter. Only I'm not gonna backslide. Never again." He wiped the back of a grimy hand across his face, leaving a faint dark smear on one cheek. "Maybe you're right. Maybe I just jumped the gun about Ginger. Ah, God, I can't stand the idea of her selling herself. It drives me crazy thinking about it."

"She loves you, you love her. Give her the benefit of the doubt."

"Yeah," he said. Then he said, "Carol. She'll know. Ginger don't have no secrets from her."

"Who's Carol?"

"Her best friend. They're like sisters. She hates my guts, not that I blame her."

"What's Carol's last name? Where does she live?"

"Why you want to know that?"

"Maybe she knows something about what happened to Janice."

"Yeah." He put a hand out, not quite touching the sleeve of my jacket. "You ask her about Ginger, too, huh? Make sure about her, let me know what she says?"

"Sure. Put your mind at ease."

"No lie? You'll let me know one way or another?"

"I'll let you know."

He nodded. All the hardness had gone out of him; he looked relieved. And sad and hurting and lost and vulnerable—a man who had hit bottom and was clawing his way back up, inch by painful inch.

"Carol Brixon," he said. "She's a bartender at the Rick-rack Lounge on Columbus. Day-shift, same as Ginger."

16

JAKE RUNYON

Sausalito was a little hillside and waterfront town filled with million-dollar homes on the Marin side of the Golden Gate Bridge. Former fishing village, artists' colony, San Francisco bedroom community, real estate agent's wet dream, and expensive tourist trap. That was as much as Runyon knew about it—as much as he wanted to know. Scenic places had no appeal to him anymore. Picturesque or nondescript or squalid, they were just places. The only things about Sausalito that registered on him were the swarming number of picture-taking, gabbling tourists that flocked the downtown streets and the difficulty in finding a legal parking space. He didn't have to worry about either one this trip.

The Wells Fargo branch where Ginny Lawson worked was on Bridgeway, on the north end of town away from the tourist clutter, and he could use the customer parking lot. Turned out she was a bank officer, occupying one of half a dozen desks on a carpeted area opposite the tellers' cages. The nameplate on the desk said VIRGINIA F. LAWSON. Nobody was in the customer chair in front it.

She glanced up from her computer screen when he sat down. Prim little professional smile. Devout and conservative, Dré Janssen had called her, and she looked it: gray skirt and jacket, white blouse, minimum amount of makeup, no cornrows or any other kind of distinctive African American hairdo. Her eyes had a remote quality, as if they were looking at you through a self-imposed filter.

"May I help you?"

"I hope so." He laid his card in front of her. "I'm not here on bank business. Private professional matter."

"Yes?" She glanced at the card, frowned, and said the word again with a flatter inflection. "Yes?"

"It's about Brian Youngblood."

She froze. Like running water suddenly turning to ice. In a strained voice she said, "I have nothing to say to anyone about Brian Youngblood."

"He's in trouble, Ms. Lawson. Maybe serious trouble."

No response. Silence built up between them, thick and heavy. It occurred to him that she intended to keep on sitting there like that, frozen and silent, until he gave it up and went away. He waited as motionlessly as she sat, holding eye contact, letting her know he wasn't leaving until she talked to him.

The silence lasted for maybe two minutes. Then, "I'm not surprised."

"That Brian is in trouble?"

"He's sick. He has been for a long time."

"Sick in what way?"

"Mentally. He's mentally ill."

"That covers a lot of territory. It might help if you'd be more specific."

Tight little headshake.

"Is that the reason you wouldn't marry him? Because you think he's mentally ill?"

"I won't discuss my private life."

"If you know something that might explain—"

"I said I won't discuss it."

"I understand it must be painful for you—"

"Don't you listen? No means no."

"Brandy," he said.

She jerked as if he'd touched her with an electrode. The tight little headshake again, then the frozen silence.

"You know her, Ms. Lawson. Tell me about her."

Nothing.

"She's part of Brian's troubles, isn't she? Maybe the root cause."

Nothing.

"Is she the reason you ended your relationship with him?"

Still nothing. But the ice was beginning to crack. She sat just as rigidly, but muscles had begun to twitch in her face—an effect like fissures forming and spreading on a glacial moraine.

"Ms. Lawson?"

She started to laugh. A low, bitter, humorless sound that caused a couple of nearby heads to turn. The facial muscles kept twitching, as if they were acting as a pump for the dribbling laughter.

"Brandy," she said. "Oh God, *Brandy*."

"Ms. Lawson?"

"Sick," she said, "sick, sick," and went right on laughing.

It was as if she were alone somewhere, all alone in a place he couldn't get to and wouldn't want to be if he could. He got up and went away from her and the empty sounds of her anguish.

B ack to the city. He took the Lincoln Boulevard exit just beyond the bridge toll plaza, wound down through the Presidio past Baker Beach and Sea Cliff and over to Lake Street. Brian Youngblood's former girlfriend Verna Washington had recently moved from the Haight to an apartment on Lake, but stopping there was a wasted effort: she wasn't home. Already at Bon Chance, the downtown French restaurant where she worked as pastry chef? He called the restaurant number. She wasn't there, either.

Getting on toward noon. His schedule was open until two o'clock, and he wasn't hungry. Bill had the Nick Kinsella lead covered, and Tamara had been in touch with Rose Youngblood to report on progress, or the lack of it, so far. Which left him with Aaron Myers.

He called Fresh To You Frozen Foods. Myers was out of the office again today. Home ill with the flu, the woman who answered told him; might not be back at his desk again until next week. Did he want to be connected to Mr. Myers's voice mail? No, he didn't.

Runyon drove down Lake, took Divisidero south to

Castro, and went along there into Noe Valley. He leaned on Aaron Myers's doorbell for two minutes without getting a response. Too sick to answer, maybe. Or maybe his illness was an excuse to take a few days off work for reasons of his own.

Another talk with Brian Youngblood? Might as well give it a shot. If the man was alone, without Brandy to intimidate him, he might be induced to give out with some straight answers.

He drove up to Duncan Street. Another waste of time. No answer to another couple of minutes of bell-ringing. It went like that sometimes; people not home, unavailable, information hard to come by and sketchy when you did manage to pry some loose.

Now what?

He should have gone downtown to make sure he was on time for his two o'clock appointment. But he didn't. Without making a conscious decision, he drove up and over Twin Peaks and west to Nineteenth Avenue. When he got to Moraga, he turned off and circled down to Bryn Darby's address.

Small, single-family home, brown-shingled, not much larger than a cottage tucked between a larger house and a two-story apartment building. Strip of browning lawn and some kind of flowering shrub in front. Security gate across the front porch. Drawn venetian blinds over the facing windows. No sign of the chocolate-covered Scion anywhere on the block.

At the corner he made a U-turn, drove slowly until he neared her house, then braked and pulled over to the curb opposite. And sat there looking across at the house. Not thinking about anything, just sitting and looking for three or four minutes with the engine running. Then he switched it off, opened the door, and started to get out. But that was as far as he got. Duty rather than propriety stopped him: he was going to be late for his two o'clock appointment as it was and he hated being late. He slid back under the wheel, fired up the engine again. Before he drove away he shut himself down all the way, so he was not thinking at all.

17

The big hype is that cell phones are one of the wonders of the modern age. Bells and whistles galore. You can talk to others, receive voice and text messages, send text messages, take photographs, play music and games, access your e-mail, and, for all I know, track the progress of herds of elephants on the African veldt. All in one self-contained little unit that fits in your shirt pocket and the palm of your hand. Some people seem to worship the things; they're the ones you see every day on streets and highways and sidewalks and in public buildings with cells glued to their ears and rapt, satisfied expressions on their faces. Instant telecommunication orgasms delivered by your choice of jaunty, sappy tunes and other fun electronic noises.

Not for me.

For me, they're a sometimes useful business tool and a pain in the ass.

No photograph has ever been taken or text message sent on mine. I don't have e-mail to access—Tamara and Kerry take care of my needs on that score—or interest in any of the other options. And I've never felt the desire for constant connection to my loved ones, business acquaintances, casual friends, and total strangers. A phone, in my old-fashioned world, is an instrument that provides necessary—emphasis on the word *necessary*—access to another person for a definite purpose. It is not a toy. It is not a source of public auditory (or visual) masturbation. Above all, it should not be, but too often is, an annoying, attention-distracting, accident-causing, self-indulgent plaything used at others' expense.

Two other negative aspects of cell phones. The battery usually runs down when you need it the most and you're someplace far away from the charger, and the thing then beeps and burbles at you until you shut it off—if you can figure out how to shut it off. And it invariably rings at the most inconvenient time. All phones ring at inconvenient times now and then, but cells seem to be the worst offenders by far. Mine is, anyway. Mine is controlled by gremlins. If I'm at the office or at home, or someplace waiting quietly for a call, it never rings. It seems to go off only when I'm in the car driving. If I get ten calls a week, that's when nine of them will come in. This doesn't seem to bother most drivers; you see them everywhere with one hand clapped to an ear, mouths moving like mental cases muttering to themselves in locked rooms. There was a new law in California against this, as there is in New York and other states, but it had yet to be enacted and even when it was, the cell phone junkies would ignore it and the law would play hell trying to enforce it. Once you give people a fancy new toy, you'd better not try to take it away from them; it produces tantrums, and in adults tantrums can sometimes be accompanied by guns, knives, and other deadly weapons.

What set me off on this frustrated internal rant was not one, not two, not three, but four incoming calls while I was making the cross-city drive from the Outer Mission to North Beach. Time-consuming, every one, because I refuse to talk while driving and so I had to pull over each time to answer. I could have let the calls go onto voice mail, but I'm not made that way, either. Phone rings, you pick up. Might be important. You never know.

I was on Mission near Army, headed east, when the first one came in. Mitchell Krochek. He'd gone to his house on his lunch hour, he said. Still no sign of his wife, still no messages. Had I found out anything yet? No? He started in on another of his this-waiting-is-driving-me-crazy laments, and I cut him off, not as tactfully as I might have, in the middle of it.

No sooner had I pulled out into traffic and beat a yellow light at the intersection than the phone rang again. Tamara this time. She said, "Guess who just called?"

"The idiot in the White House. He wants my input on gay marriage."

"Funny, but wrong. Guess again."

"Enough guessing. Who called?"

"Carl Lassiter."

"Well, well," I said. "So word got back to him. Quilmes, probably."

"Looks that way."

"What'd he have to say?"

"Wanted to talk to you. I told him you were out of the

office and unavailable. So he asked me why we were investigating him and QCL, Inc. Not hostile—real polite and businesslike. I told him we weren't, just that their names'd come up in the course of another investigation."

"And he asked what that was and you said it was confidential."

"You got it. Wanted to know when could he see you. I told him I didn't know, I'd have to call him back. Gave me his cell number and said ASAP."

"That's all right with me. But let's dangle him a little. Tell him not until five o'clock, so he has to fight the rush hour traffic."

"Here?"

"Nowhere else. Make him come to us."

The third call arrived about four minutes later, as I was trying to maneuever around a stalled Muni bus on Mission and Twenty-second. The thing jangled five times before I could get around the bus and into a yellow zone on the next block. I growled a hello, and Kerry said, "Well, don't bite my head off."

"Sorry. I'm in the car fighting traffic. What's up?"

Nothing was up. The late-scheduled meeting at Bates and Carpenter had been canceled, so she'd be able to pick up Emily at her music class after all. Okay by me. Parenthood for the first time at our ages carries a lot more responsibility, compromise, and time-juggling than you consider going in, even when one of the parents is supposed to be semiretired. Semiretirement, for me these days, seemed to mean working as many hours as I had when I ran the agency single-handed.

I was downtown when the damn phone went off for the fourth time. Somebody from the Blacklight Tavern who didn't give his name. One-line message: Mr. Kinsella was in his office now and he'd see me anytime before three o'clock, the sooner the better, he was a busy man.

Yeah. Me, too. But all right. North Beach and Carol Brixon could go on hold. I don't like jumping when men like Kinsella snap their fingers, but I was the one currying favor here. Bite the bullet and get it over with.

The Blacklight Tavern was on San Bruno Avenue, off Bayshore west of Candlestick Park. One of the city's older residential neighborhoods, working-class, like the one I'd grown up in. During World War II, and while the Hunters Point Naval Shipyard humped along for twenty-five years afterward, it had been a reasonably decent section to raise a family in. But then the shipyard shut down, and mostly black Hunters Point began to deteriorate into a mean-streets ghetto. Now, with the gang-infested Point on one side and the drug deli that McLaren Park had degenerated into on the other, the neighborhood had suffered badly. Signs of decay were everywhere: boarded-up storefronts, bars on windows and doors, houses disfigured by graffiti and neglect, homeless people and drunks huddled in doorways.

Kinsella's domain fit right in. From a distance it looked like something that had been badly scorched in a fire. Black-painted facade, smoke-tinted windows, black sign with neon letters that would blaze white after dark but looked burned-out in the daylight. No graffiti. None of the neighborhood taggers would dare deface those black walls. Nick Kinsella had a big, bad rep out here; even the drug-dealing gangs left him and his people alone.

I parked in front and locked the car out of habit. It was safe enough here, this close to the Blacklight; in the next block it would've been fair game for anybody who thought it contained something tradeable for a rock of crack or a jug of cheap wine. Inside, the place might've been any down-scale neighborhood bar populated by the usual array of day-time drinkers. A couple of the men and one of the women gave me bleary-eyed once-overs, decided I wasn't anybody worth knowing, hustling, or hassling, and turned their attention back to the focal point of their lives. The bartender, a barrel-shaped guy with a head like a redwood burl and a surly manner, was the same one who'd been on duty the last time I was here. If he recognized me when I bellied up, he gave no indication of it. All he said was, "Yeah?"

"Nick Kinsella. He's expecting me."

"Name?"

I told him. He said, "Just a minute," and used the phone on the backbar. When he came back he said, "Okay. First door past the ladies' crapper."

"I know where it is."

I went and knocked on the door and walked in. Mostly barren office that reeked of cigar smoke and had two men in it, Kinsella and one of his enforcers, a lopsided, balding guy with the build of a wrestler whose name I didn't know. Kinsella sat bulging behind a cherrywood desk. He'd grown a third chin since I'd last seen him, added another junk-food inch or two to his waistline.

"Long time, Nick."

"Long time," he agreed. "How's it hangin'?"

"Short, like always."

He thought that was funny. The enforcer didn't crack a smile.

Kinsella said, "So what brings you around this time? Don't tell me you got money troubles?"

"Not your kind."

"So?"

"Just some information. Maybe I can give you some in return."

"Yeah? Like what?"

"About one of your competitors."

One bushy eyebrow lifted. "Who'd that be?"

"QCL, Incorporated."

"Never heard of 'em."

"Carl Lassiter."

"Never heard of him."

Good. Trade material. It's always easier to deal with the slimeball element when you know something they don't. I said, "All right if I sit down?"

He waved a fat hand at the only other chair. "Sure, sure, sit." And I when I was on the chair, "So what about this guy Lassiter?"

"He works for QCL. Quick Cash Loans. It's a Vegas outfit."

"Vegas?"

"With branch reps in half a dozen other cities, including S.F. High-interest loans to gamblers and prostitution on the side."

"The hell you say."

"So this is all news to you."

"Yeah, news. Tell me more about this outfit."

I told him all I knew. He soaked it up; you could almost see the wheels turning in his head.

"Sounds like a smart operation," he said. "Low pressure, no overhead. Big profits, huh?"

"Probably."

"But they only work the gambling trade. That don't cut much into *my* profits, not the way they work it. No real competition."

"But you're glad to know about them."

"Oh, yeah. Always glad to know about the competition."

"And maybe if you put out the word, you could find out a little more."

"Maybe. That what you're after, more info on this QCL?"

"One of the reasons I'm here, yeah."

"What's the other one?"

"Different case. One of your customers."

"Yeah? Who?"

"Brian Youngblood."

"Names," Kinsella said. "I got a lot of customers, I'm no good with names."

"Black guy in his twenties, works in computers, lives on Duncan Street. Five-figure borrow."

His face showed me nothing. He leaned back in his chair, clasped his sausage fingers behind his neck. "Maybe I know him, maybe I don't. How come you're so interested?"

"He's in over his head. We're trying to find out how deep."

"Working for him?"

"No."

"Who, then?"

"Confidential, Nick."

"Better not be if it's got something to do with me."

I hesitated. But you couldn't pry information out of Kinsella by holding out on him. "All right," I said. "His mother."

Kinsella's lips twitched. Don't laugh, you bastard, I thought. He didn't; he sat forward again. "I don't like to talk about my customers. Bad for business."

"Only if word gets out. I'm a businessman, too, Nick. You know I know how to keep my mouth shut."

"Just a couple of business types schmoozing, huh?"

"That's right."

"No hassles?"

"Not from me. Just trying to help a client, that's all."

He thought about it, shrugged, and said, "Okay. So what you want to know?"

"Amount of the initial borrow, if he came back for more, how much he's into you for now. And whether something can be worked out in the way of accident insurance."

"Kid already have an accident, did he?"

"Just last week. Bruises and a broken rib. Laid him up for a couple of days."

"That's too bad," Kinsella said. "But you got to expect something like that when you don't pay attention to your debts."

The fat son of a bitch was enjoying himself, playing this little game. Maybe someday I'd have a chance to play a different kind of game with him; it was a good thought and I held onto it. "The original nut," I said. "How much?"

"I'd have to check my records."

"Would you do that?"

He grinned at me. There was a computer on his desk: Nick Kinsella, the ultra-modern bloodsucker. He fired it up, looked over at me—I turned my head the other way—and then did some tapping on the keyboard. Pretty soon he said, "Five figures, right. Ten K."

"That's a big nut. What'd he use for collateral?"

"Personal property and income records. I had one of my people take a look, I was satisfied."

"What does he owe you now, with the vig and the missed payments? Thirteen, fourteen K?"

"Five."

". . . Wait a minute—five thousand? How'd he get it down that far?"

Kinsella's smug grin flashed again. "Your boy walked in here couple of days ago, laid eighty-five hundred on me. Cash. He's a good boy, your boy. Teach him a lesson, he learns real quick. He don't need any accident insurance, not for a while anyhow."

"Where'd he get the eighty-five hundred?"

"Who knows? He don't say, I don't ask."

Not from another shark, I thought, not given the size of the original nut from Nick and the fact that Kinsella had had to send out an enforcer to collect overdue payments.

Loan sharks are like their saltwater relatives: when one spills some bad blood, the rest smell it and keep their distance.

"What about the five-thousand balance?" I asked.

"What about it?"

"If his source is dry, he'll start missing payments again. Then he will need that insurance."

"Not if he shows up next week with the full five K plus the week's interest."

"He told you he was going to do that?"

"Guaranteed it." Kinsella laughed. "Swore it, in fact. You want to know what he swore it on?"

"No."

He told me anyway. "His mother. Your boy swore it on his love for his sweet old mama."

18

The Rickrack Lounge was on the corner of Columbus and Vallejo, only a few blocks from Benjy's Seven, but that was about all they had in common. Neighborhood watering hole, the Rickrack, reminiscent in its old-fashioned ambiance, if not in its clientele, of the Washington Square Bar and Grill a couple blocks in the other direction. No loud music, no topless dancers, no sad-eyed voyeurs, no shill or bouncer. No local celebrities like Washington Square attracted, just a few quiet afternoon drinkers, two of whom were playing chess on a small magnetic board. The place had once been an Italian tavern, probably owned and frequented by the ever-diminishing Italian population of North Beach; one of the walls still sported a faded Venice mural and the handful of booths had upswept gondola-style backs.

Carol Brixon was on duty, working the plank alone—a heavyset redhead with a pleasantly homely face and a no-nonsense manner. She didn't have much to say to me, fending off my questions about Ginger Benn and QCL and Carl Lassiter, until I told her Jason Benn was worried that his wife had started hooking again. That made her angry and she opened up a little.

"That bastard," she said. "If it wasn't for him and his gambling, she wouldn't've been screwing for money in the first place."

"To pay off his debts to QCL."

"Fucking bloodsuckers. They forced her into it. Jason was in so deep he'd never've got out otherwise."

"She could have just walked away from him."

"You think I didn't tell her that? Hell, I begged her. But she's loyal and she loves him. She'd rather sleep with strangers than divorce a prick."

"He seems to've gotten his act together. Working steady now, not betting anymore."

"Yeah, maybe. For Ginger's sake, I hope so. We been friends a long time, her and me. I couldn't stand to see her go back to peddling her ass."

"So she's not hooking again."

"Not that I know about."

"Do you know if she's seen Lassiter recently?"

"Better not have. Slick as a snake, that one, and just as cold."

"Sounds like you know him."

"No, and I don't want to. Only met him once, at Benjy's. I went there to meet Ginger and he was slithering around. Once was enough."

"Violent, would you say?"

"If you backed him into a corner."

"But not otherwise? No physical stuff to keep women like Ginger in line?"

"Not him. Just his mouth, that's all he uses—all he needs."

"And it's just him running the show here, no people working for him?"

"Just him."

"Any violent types among the customers?"

She gave me one of those looks old-time San Franciscans reserve for visitors from red-state backwaters. "We work in the bar trade, mister. There's *always* some macho asshole around flexing his muscles."

"I meant among the johns Lassiter pimps for. Any of them ever get rough with Ginger?"

"Why don't you ask her?"

"She won't talk to me about QCL or Lassiter."

"Yeah, well, I shouldn't be talking to you, either. You show me a license, you act like one of the good guys, but how do I know?"

"You don't. Look at this face, take it on faith."

A smile tickled one corner of her mouth. She leaned over, gave the bartop in front of me a fast polish.

"*Did* Ginger have trouble with any of her johns?"

"What kind of trouble? Smack her around, you mean?"

"Anything that involves violence."

"No. I don't think so. She wouldn't stand for crap like that."

"She'd have told you if she had?"

"She'd've told me. Yeah. No secrets between us."

"One more question. The woman I'm looking for, Janice Stanley. Are you sure you've never met her?"

"Positive," Carol Brixon said. "Ginger didn't tell me she had a roommate. Subject never came up."

Another dead end. I seemed to be learning plenty about how QCL worked its scams, but not getting any closer to finding out who beat up Janice Stanley Krochek or what had happened to her.

Carl Lassiter was already there when I walked into the agency at twenty till five. Sitting on the anteroom couch, one leg crossed, fingers interlaced on his knee—picture of a man at ease. When he saw me he unfolded, slowly, to his feet. There was a lot of him to unfold. About six-two and a solid two hundred and ten pounds, most of it encased in a silky brown suit that must have cost a couple of grand. Thick gold ring with a diamond setting on one hand, a gold stickpin in his Sulka tie. Freshly barbered look, wavy sand-colored hair styled to a fault. Suave little smile on a thinnish mouth. But none of that disguised what he was underneath. Carol Brixon had described him perfectly: slick as a snake and just as cold.

Tamara's office door was open; she came out to stand framed in it. The set of her jaw and the downturn of her mouth told me what she thought of him.

He said my name in the form of a question. I admitted it. He said, "Carl Lassiter," and put out his hand. I ignored it, watching his eyes. Chips of blue ice. But the suave little smile stayed put.

"Nice offices you have here," he said.

Tamara said, "They were until about ten minutes ago."

Lassiter ignored her as pointedly as I'd ignored his hand. "Is there somewhere we can talk privately?" he said to me.

"My office."

I took him in there. The connecting door was shut; Tamara's outer door slammed as I closed mine.

"Feisty little gal you've got there," Lassiter said. "You should teach her to be more polite."

"She's polite enough when the situation warrants it," I said. "And she happens to be my partner. You saw the names on the door."

"Pretty young for your kind of work, isn't she?"

"Old enough."

"So are you," Lassiter said. "Is it all right if I sit down?"

"Help yourself."

Both of us sat. When he saw that I wasn't going to bite on the "So are you" line, he followed it up himself. "Old enough to know better than to ask questions about things that don't concern you."

"Anything that concerns a case I'm working on concerns me."

"Just what case are you working on?"

"As Ms. Corbin told you, that's confidential information."

He said, parroting me, "Anything that concerns my company concerns me."

"This particular investigation doesn't concern you or your company. At least not directly, so far as I can tell right now."

"So you're not investigating me?"

"Not you, and not QCL, Incorporated."

"Then why the heat?"

"What heat?"

"Asking questions about us, bothering people associated with us."

"That's not heat. Stepping on your toes a little, maybe."

"Whatever you want to call it. Why?"

"We're an investigative agency, Mr. Lassiter. We ask a lot of questions of a lot of people. We step on a lot of toes, too, unintentionally most of the time."

"But not all the time."

"No. Not all the time."

He studied his fingernails, polished one set on the leg of his slacks, studied them again. Very nonchalant, very much in control. But he was steaming underneath. In this business you learn to read people's body language and emotional barometer, some more easily than others. He was one of the easy ones.

"What's your interest in Jorge Quilmes?" Casual, offhand, as if he were asking about the weather.

"No interest, specifically."

"Ginger Benn."

"Same answer."

"Janice Stanley."

Now we were getting down to it. I said, "She was Ginger Benn's roommate this past month. At your request, I understand."

"Who told you that? Ginger?"

"No."

"Who, then?"

"Was it supposed to be a secret?"

"Of course not. I'm curious, that's all."

"Sorry," I said. "Confidential."

"All right." He bit that off a little short. But he was still smiling when he said, "Suppose we dispense with the bullshit."

"I'm always in favor of that."

"Janice Stanley turned up missing and you're looking for her. You think I had something to do with her disappearance?"

"Did you?"

"Of course not."

"But she was working for you at the time."

"Working for me?"

"For QCL then. Hooking for QCL."

"That's a ridiculous statement," Lassiter said. "We're in the business of lending money, nothing more."

"That's not the way I heard it."

"You think we're pimps, is that it?"

"For a highly specialized clientele."

"Even if it were true, you couldn't prove it."

"I'm not interested in proving it."

"No? What are you interested in?"

"Doing the job I was hired to do."

"Finding Janice Stanley."

"You wouldn't have any idea of where she is, would you?"

"No. I'd tell you if I did."

"Sure you would. When did you see her last?"

He thought the question over before he answered it. "Last week sometime. I don't remember the exact day."

"Friday, Saturday?"

"Before that. Early part of the week."

"Talk to her after that?"

"No."

"She have any dates scheduled after the one with Jorge Quilmes?"

"Now how would I know that?" he said through his cocky little smile.

"Somebody used her for a punching bag on the weekend."

"Is that right? Sorry to hear it."

"Could've been one of her johns."

"Johns? She's a prostitute, is she?"

"Call girl. I understand there's a lot of money in that kind of work."

"I wouldn't know."

"Could also have been someone she knows, someone who set up her dates for her."

"We're back to that again. Back to me."

"I'm just tossing out possibilities."

"Prostitutes get beat up all the time," Lassiter said. "Sometimes by their husbands, if they have husbands."

"Doesn't apply in this case."

"Are you sure of that?"

"Pretty sure," I said.

"Then there're the creeps," he said. "Could be one of them."

"Creeps?"

"You know, the ones who think any hooker is fair game—hassle them looking to get laid. Have you considered that possibility?"

I said, "Maybe I should."

He said, "There's one like that in the place she was staying."

". . . The Hillman? Who?"

"Desk clerk. Redhaired little punk named Phil."

"He hassled Janice Stanley?"

"I wouldn't know about that."

"Ginger Benn, then. That you do know about."

He shrugged.

"She give in to him? No, she wouldn't. Not her."

"I wouldn't bother her about it," Lassiter said. "If I were you, I wouldn't bother Mr. Quilmes or any of his friends anymore, either."

"Or you or QCL."

"That's right. Keep off toes that might just get sore enough to start kicking back."

"Is that a threat, Mr. Lassiter?"

"I don't make threats. Merely offering some friendly advice."

Enough. I didn't want to play with him anymore. I said, "I'll keep it under advisement," and got to my feet.

"You do that. Don't forget."

"I won't. I won't forget you, either."

"Same here."

Lassiter stood up slowly, the way he had in the ante-room. The smile was still in place, but a little less suave, a little less cocky. He gave me a mock salute and went out, leaving the door open, in a kind of lazy saunter like a man without a care in the world. But it was pose and pretense now. He was still steaming, still worried underneath.

I sat down again. The tight little confrontation had accomplished something positive, by God. You spend a couple of days running around, talking to a variety of people, and not getting anywhere on the Krochek disappearance, and the one man you least expect to be of help drops the best lead yet right into your lap. And as a throwaway, no less. Lassiter hadn't been trying to give me anything when he brought up the Hillman desk clerk; on the contrary, he'd intended it as a red herring to focus my attention somewhere other than on him and QCL, Inc.

The connecting door opened. Tamara said, "I was listening."

"I figured you would be."

"That's one sleazy dude under all that cool. You think he's dangerous?"

"Probably. But not to us."

"So what're you going to do?"

"About Lassiter?"

"Him and QCL."

"Turn over what we've got on them, and anything else Kinsella can dig up, to Jake Logan at SFPD. He can pass it on down to Vice. Not much they can do unless Lassiter steps out of line somehow or one of the victims turns on him, but at least they'll have the information on file."

"Ginger Benn, you think?"

"Doubtful. Too afraid of what might happen to her husband. I don't see Janice Krochek doing it, either—if she's still alive."

"She'd've turned up by now if she was."

"You'd think so. What worries me is that she might never turn up again at all, alive or dead."

Jake Runyon showed up just then and poked his head through the door of my office. "Just the man I wanted to see," I said. "I was about to give you a call."

"What's up?"

"Couple of things. Your pro bono case, for one—I had a talk with Nick Kinsella. The Krochek disappearance, for another. How'd you like to take a ride, put in some over-time?"

"Okay with me. Where're we going?"

"The Hillman. I'll fill you in on the way."

19

There was a different clerk behind the desk when Runyon and I walked into the lobby. Thin, middle-aged, dour. "Phil Partain?" he said. "His shift ends at five. You friends of his?"

"Personal business," I said.

"Uh-huh. He don't have many friends."

"Where can we find him?"

"I think he went out to eat . . . No, he didn't. Pretty sure I saw him get into the elevator and he hasn't come down yet."

"Where'd he go?"

"His room."

"He lives here, does he? How about that."

"Yeah. You want me to call up, make sure he's in?"

"No," I said, "we'll just go on up and see. What's the room number?"

"Four-twelve. Top floor, rear."

A bulb was out in the section of the fourth floor hallway where 412 was situated. It was the last room at the end of a short ell that reeked of disinfectant. There was no peephole in the panel, just the numerals. I ran my knuckles against the door in a steady tattoo until Partain's voice said irritably, "All right, all right. Who is it?"

Neither Runyon nor I answered. I kept knocking until the lock clicked and the door swung inward and Partain appeared, saying, "For Chrissake, what's the idea—" The rest of it died in his throat when he saw us standing there.

"Let's have a little talk, Phil."

"Why? What do you want?"

"Inside, where it's private."

"No. You can't come busting in—"

We could and we did, crowding him backward. Runyon shut the door and stood with his back against it. My show; Jake was there to make it a power play, two against one.

The apartment was small, two rooms and bath, and a sour-smelling mess of strewn clothing, dirty dishes, empty takeout food containers. A flickery TV set tuned to a sports show yammered in one corner. The hot plate on a table by one wall had caused a fire at some point; the section of wall behind and above it was scorched. Partain was in his underwear, T-shirt and shorts both yellowed and baggy. He backed off from us, stopped in the middle of the room, and stood with his skinny, hairless legs spread and his hands on his hips and his jaw outthrust—the picture of belligerent indignation.

"What the hell's the idea?" he demanded. "You can't just push your way into a man's room . . ."

"We didn't," I said. "You invited us."

"Bullshit. What you guys want?"

"The answers to some questions. Straight answers."

"Questions about what?"

"Janice Stanley," I said.

His head twitched slightly; his eyes flicked aside, flicked back to meet mine again. "I already told you, I don't know nothing about her."

"I think maybe you do."

"Yeah, well, you're wrong."

"She disappeared sometime Tuesday. Hasn't been seen since."

"Christ, what's that have to do with me?"

"The last time you saw her—when was that again?"

"I don't remember. Last week sometime."

"Last Saturday?"

"No. Before that."

"You told me you saw her on Saturday."

"Might've been Saturday, I don't know. My memory's not so good—"

"How about Sunday? You see her Sunday?"

"No."

He said that too fast, too emphatically. Flat-out lie.

"Sure you did, Phil. Where was it? In the lobby?"

"Don't you listen? I don't work Sundays."

"Don't go out, either, not even to eat?"

"At night. I was here all day, right here watching TV."

"So this is where you saw Janice Stanley. She dropped by for a visit, is that it?"

"No!"

Another lie. There were oily pearls of sweat on Partain's forehead now. His face had a grayish cast.

"Must be you invited her, then," I said.

"How many times I have to tell you? She wasn't here, I never saw her Sunday."

"Why lie about it, Phil? If you had a date with her, why not just tell us?"

"I never had a date with her. A whore? You think I make dates with whores?"

"How do you know she's a whore?"

"I know what goes on around here. Her and that Ginger Benn—"

"You think Ginger's a whore, too?"

"Damn right she is."

"If either of them was hooking," I said, "it was probably a call-girl kind of thing. Expensive. Discreet. No johns in the apartment here."

"I got eyes, I got ears—Hey, what're you doing? That's private."

That last was directed at Runyon. He'd left the door to wander casually around the small room looking at this and that, and he'd stopped next to a pile of video cassettes and DVDs. He picked up a handful, glanced at the titles.

"Porn," he said.

"So what?" Partain said nervously. "Lots of people watch porn flicks, so what?"

"S&M, looks like."

"Everybody isn't into S&M," I said.

"I'm not into it, I just like to watch it sometimes . . ."

"But you don't do it yourself."

"No. Never."

"And you don't date whores or call girls."

"No, no, I told you—"

"You tried to date Ginger Benn."

"That's a lie! Who told you that?"

"A reliable source. You know what I think? I think you hit on Janice Stanley sometime Saturday or Sunday and she surprised you by saying yes. She needed money and she didn't much care how she got it. She'd have gone with you for the right price."

"No, no . . ."

"I think she came up here sometime on Sunday and the two of you got it on. Only you like it rough and things got out of hand—"

"No! It wasn't like that!"

"Then how was it? Why'd you beat her up?"

Partain licked his lips, waggled his head from one side to another, big-eyed, as if looking for a way out.

"Answer me, Phil. Why did you beat her up?"

"She . . . I . . . all right, all right, I caught her trying to steal money out of my wallet, all right? Afterward, after I already paid her the fifty she asked for. All right? You satisfied now?"

"You must've been damn angry. She was banged up pretty good."

"Bitch fought me, what else could I do? Tried to scratch me, kick me in the nuts. It was self-defense."

"What time did all this take place?"

"I dunno what time, late afternoon . . ."

"And then what happened?"

"What you think happened? I threw her ass out."

"And she went back to Ginger Benn's apartment."

212 • Bill Pronzini

"Yeah, I guess so. That's the last time I saw her—"

"You're lying, Phil. Ginger Benn was there on Sunday and she didn't see Janice Stanley. Nobody saw Janice until Monday morning."

"I don't know where she went, how the hell would I know?"

I was remembering those red chafe marks on Janice Krochek's wrists. "Let's try this on for size. You caught her stealing from your wallet, beat her up when she fought you, but you were still pissed and you figured it wasn't enough payback. So you held her here against her will, tied her to the bed, let's say, and used her while she was lying there helpless, and kept her tied up and kept using her until Monday morning."

It was the right scenario or close to it. Partain looked sick and panicky. Nerves jumped and crawled in his cheeks like worms under thin white latex.

"And then maybe you decided you wanted more sex, more payback. So you went over to her house on Tuesday, caught her there alone—"

"House? What house?"

"You know where she lives. You could've found out easily enough. You went over there, caught her alone—"

"I don't know what you're talking about."

"—and she gave you more trouble and things got out of hand. Is that about how it happened?"

"No!"

"Where is she, Phil? What'd you do with her body?"

"Her . . . body? Jesus, you think I . . . Jesus!"

"An accident, right? You didn't mean to kill her—"

"You're crazy! I never went to no house, I never killed nobody! You're trying to frame me, you . . ." The last word caught in his throat; he gagged, coughed up another stream of words. "I can't listen to no more of this, I don't have to stand here half-naked listening to this shit."

Partain stumbled over to an open closet door, dragged a pair of pants off a hanger. He was still at the closet door when he got them on, and when he reached in again I thought it was for a shirt. Wrong. What he was after was on the shelf above.

Gun. Stubby, scratched up Saturday night special.

I froze. So did Runyon. Partain waved the piece back and forth between us, his hand shaking hard enough to make the muzzle bob up and down. "All right, you bastards," he said, "all right!"

Both Runyon and I had been under the gun before, a couple of times together before this, and I'd been shot once a long time ago. But you never get used to looking down the bore. And the reaction, for me, is always the same: muscles bunching up tight, senses sharpening, a kind of cold calm descending over a thin layer of fear. The fear comes from uncertainty more than anything else; you can't predict what somebody with a gun in his hand will do, and that goes double for a man in the throes of panic.

I said slowly and evenly, "You want to be careful with that, Phil."

"You're not gonna arrest me, frame me for something I didn't do."

"Nobody's trying to frame you."

"I never killed that bitch Janice. I never went to her

house, I never saw her again after I threw her outta here
Monday morning."

"I believe you. Put the gun down, you don't want to
shoot anybody."

"I don't want to but I will. I'm not going to jail for
something I didn't do."

"You don't have to go to jail. If Janice Stanley's alive and
intended to press charges, she'd've done it already. You're
home free, Phil. Unless you pull that trigger and one of us
gets hurt."

It didn't register; he wasn't tracking clearly. He waved
the gun, holding it in both hands now to steady his grip.
"Get out of my way. I'm getting out of here."

Partain moved and I moved, hands up at the level of my
shoulders, palms outward. His attention was caught on
me. Runyon was a short distance away, on his left and
slightly behind him. When I saw Jake slide a careful step
forward I knew what he was going to do and I tried to
warn him off with my eyes, but he was focused on the gun.
Partain kept coming and I kept gliding aside to clear his
path to the door. He was between the two of us, starting to
glance Runyon's way as if he'd just remembered him, when
Jake made his play.

He was good and he was fast; Partain had no time to
swing the gun. Runyon judo-chopped his forearm, hit him
with the other shoulder at the same time. The Saturday
night special went spinning out of Partain's hand, clattered
on the floor. The force of the shoulder blow threw him
staggering in my direction. I couldn't get out of his way;
he caromed off me, shoving with his hands. Runyon

lunged at him, but his feet got tangled in the threadbare carpet and he tripped, lost his balance, banged a knee on the floor with enough force to bring a grunt of pain out of him. By the time he shoved up again, Partain had the door open and was out into the hall, running.

Runyon went after him. I yelled, "Jake, don't!" but he kept going. Nothing for me to do then but to join the chase. But not until I'd scooped up the weapon and slid it into my coat pocket.

When I got into the hall, Runyon was just limping around the corner ell. It took me four or five seconds to get there and take myself around it. The long hall to the elevator was empty, but I could hear running steps close by. A door halfway along was just closing on its pneumatic tube. I yanked it open and bulled through. Fire stairs. But the running steps were going up, not down.

One flight to the roof. The door at the top of the landing stood half-open; I had a glimpse of Runyon's back going through. I went running up the stairs. Not the man I used to be: I was puffing hard when I came out onto the roof.

Rough, tarry surface, heater vents and chimneys, taller buildings on all sides. And Partain at the far end, heading for a pair of curved hand bars at the top of a fire escape, and Runyon hobbling behind him. I sucked enough cold air into my lungs to yell, "Jake, let him go!" If he heard me, he kept going anyway.

Partain reached the hand bars, swung a leg over the parapet, and scrambled down out of sight.

I yelled it again, louder: "Jake! Let him go!"

It got through to him this time, broke his stride. He

looked over his shoulder, saw me gesturing, and slowed to a walk. He was at the thigh-high parapet, leaning on the hand bars and looking down, when I reached him. I don't like heights, but I eased forward to take a look myself. Partain was down past the third floor, running blindly and with enough panic to skid and bang precariously into the iron railings. He almost went over at the second floor level, caught himself just in time.

"No point in chasing him," I said.

"Guess you're right." Runyon leaned down to rub his knee. "My bad leg, dammit. I'd've caught him if I hadn't tripped."

"Doesn't matter. He's got nowhere to go that he can't be found. We've got nothing on him anyway except threat of bodily harm, and it's his word against ours on that."

"What about the gun?"

I took the Saturday night special out, broke it open. "Not even loaded."

"Shit."

That was a word Runyon hardly ever used. I glanced at him. Tight-lipped, eyes bleak and underslung with bags. Something bothering him. It could have been the hassle with Partain, but I had the sense that it went deeper than that. No use in asking; he was as closed-off a man as I'd ever known.

We started back across the roof. Runyon said, "You believe he had nothing to do with the Krochek woman's disappearance?"

"Yeah, I do. He ran because he was afraid of taking the fall for something heavier than assault and false imprisonment. He's a sorry little son of a bitch, but he's not a kid-napper or a murderer."

"Then who's responsible?"

"Well, like it or not," I said, "there's one person left we haven't taken a good long look at. Her husband—our client."

20

JAKE RUNYON

When he left the Hillman, he knew he should start following up on what Bill had told him about Nick Kinsella and the eighty-five hundred dollars Brian Youngblood had paid on his debt. But the skirmish with Phil Partain had left a sour taste; he was done with business for the day. He drove straight up over Twin Peaks and west to the brown-shingled house on Moraga Street.

He didn't even try to talk himself out of it. He was going to see Bryn Darby sooner or later, and it might as well be right away, tonight, if she was home. This crazy damn compulsion was like a fever in his blood and the only way to get rid of it was to face her, let her tell him to leave her alone, let her shame him into it. What other reaction could she have, some guy she'd seen once in her life obsessing over her? Yell at him, call him names—that was what he wanted her to do.

Wasn't it?

He didn't know. Goddamn it, he'd always known what he wanted. Now all of a sudden he wasn't sure anymore.

Yes, he was: he wanted the past, not the present and sure as hell not the future. He wanted Colleen to still be alive, he wanted his old life in Seattle back, he wanted to be a part of his son's life. But the past was dead, irretrievable. All he had was the present, and the present didn't include Joshua—the present was his work, nothing more. Only now there was this crap with Bryn Darby, whatever it was, to complicate what needed to be simple. He *had* to put an end to it one way or another, drive it out of himself, so he could get back to where he was before last Friday night: a tightly wrapped detective with all his emotional baggage carefully stowed so he wouldn't stumble over it.

She was home; lights glowed behind drawn blinds in one of the brown-shingled house's front windows. He squeezed the Ford into a narrow space between two driveways a short distance beyond. It was a cold night, the wind biting out here near the ocean, but he could feel sweat starting under his armpits as he walked back. Crazy, he thought. He forced the shutters up in his mind, got a tight grip on himself. Climbed the stairs and rang the bell.

Nothing for several seconds. Then footfalls and a guarded woman's voice behind the closed door. "Yes? Who is it?"

"Mrs. Darby? Bryn Darby?"

"Yes?"

"My name is Runyon, Jake Runyon. Last Friday night at Safeway . . . I'm the man who helped you."

She said, "Oh," faintly and there was a long pause. "What do you want?"

"A few minutes of your time, that's all."

Another, shorter pause. Then the porch light came on, a deadbolt lock rattled, and the door opened on a chain. The good side of her face peered out at him warily.

His mind had gone suddenly blank. He said the first words that came to him, "I hope I'm not interrupting your dinner . . ."

"It's too early for my dinner. How did you find out where I live?"

"It's what I do. My job."

"I don't understand."

"Finding people. I'm a detective."

"Detective? Police?"

"No." He had his license case in his hand; he flipped it open and held it up close to the opening. "Private investigator."

The visible eye blinked. It was a darker brown than he remembered, the iris very large, the lashes above it long and feathery. The suffering in it was as he remembered, too. Like something alive and hurt, hiding in a dark place.

"Is it trouble about what happened?"

"No," he said, "nothing like that."

"I don't . . . have I done something?"

"No."

"They why are you here? Do you want something from me?"

"No."

"Payment of some kind for your help?"

He shook his head.

The eye narrowed anyway. The smooth skin along her cheek tightened until the cheekbone stood out in shadowed relief. "Like for instance a date?"

"I don't . . . Date?"

"Divorced woman and damaged goods besides," she said with brittle irony. "Ought to be grateful, right? Easy pickings."

"No, you're wrong. That's not it at all."

"Isn't it?"

The cynicism in her voice was a small, cold thing surrounded by the hurt. Her pain had sharpened; the radiating force of it backed him up a pace. Made him feel ashamed, too—the self-recriminative feeling he craved. He shook his head again. "I'm sorry," he said, "I never meant to hurt you, I don't want to hurt you anymore," and he swung around and went quickly down the stairs.

He was nearing the sidewalk when he heard the door chain rattle, her voice saying, "Wait," then her steps on the porch. He stopped. She was tying one of her scarves around her head, covering the frozen side of her face, as she came down. No coat, only a thin sweater over an ankle-length skirt, but she'd taken the time to grab the scarf on her way out.

She stood off from him at the foot of the stairs, her body turned so that the shielded side of her face was out of his line of vision. "If you're really not after something, why did you bother to track me down?"

"I don't know," he said.

"That's not an answer. You must have some idea."

"A compulsion, that's all. At Safeway, the way you looked . . ."

"I know how I look."

"That's not what I meant."

"What did you mean?"

Another headshake. He couldn't seem to control the muscles in his neck. "You don't have to wear that scarf," he said. "Or stand like that, turned to the side."

"Yes, I do. What're you going to say now? That you're sorry about my deformity but I should learn to deal with it?"

"I'd never say that."

"You don't know anything about what happened to me . . . Or do you? Did you track that down, too—my entire medical history?"

"No."

"But you do know what happened."

"A little. Not much."

"And you want to know more, is that it? Diseases can be *so* interesting."

This time he managed not to move his head. He said nothing.

She came a step closer, as if on the same impulse that had brought her out of the house. "You said you didn't want to hurt me anymore. What did you mean by that? How could you hurt me?"

"By coming here like this, bothering you."

The visible side of her mouth formed a bitter smile. "This is nothing. I've been hurt a lot worse."

"I know," he said.

"You know? No, you don't. You can't imagine."

"I think I can."

"From a few facts you dug up about me?"

"Not from facts. I knew it at Safeway, when I saw you up close. I could see it, feel it."

"Bullshit," she said.

"It's the truth."

"I suppose you're psychic."

"No. It's just that I recognize pain when I see it."

"Oh, you do? Now you're going to tell me you've been hurt, too."

"Yes. I have."

"How?"

"It doesn't matter."

"You look perfectly healthy to me."

"It had nothing to do with my health."

"Somebody else's?"

"My wife's." He had no intention of saying the words, but they came out anyway. Like something solid tearing at his throat. "She died."

Bryn Darby stood quiet for several seconds. The cold wind tore at the silence between them, made her shiver; she crossed her arms tight across her breasts. "When?" she said.

"Nearly two years ago. Ovarian cancer."

"I'm sorry."

"So am I."

More silence. He wanted to leave, but his body wouldn't let him. His bad leg and sore knee began to ache.

Abruptly she said, "You're lonely."

He didn't respond.

"That's it, isn't it? The reason you're here. You're lonely."

"No," he said.

"Yes, you are. I can see it in your face."

He didn't deny it this time.

"And you think I'm lonely. Kindred spirits."

He hadn't thought that. He hadn't let himself think it.

"It wouldn't work," she said.

"What wouldn't?"

"You, me, a couple of damaged strangers crying on each other's shoulders. It wouldn't work."

He heard himself say, "I just thought . . . Talk a little, that's all."

"No," she said.

"Public place. Over coffee or a meal."

"I'm sorry, no. It wouldn't do either of us any good. And I don't want anyone in my life right now, not old friends and certainly not a new one like you. You understand?"

"Yes," he said.

"You'd better go." She hugged herself tighter. "It's cold out here."

"I won't bother you again, Mrs. Darby."

"I'm not Mrs. Darby. Not anymore, thank God." She turned and went back up the stairs. He was moving away when she called after him, "I hope you find someone else."

He didn't want anyone else, he wanted Colleen. *You're lonely. And you think I'm lonely. Kindred spirits.* All right. He was lonely, there was no denying it. Companionship, love? All the things he'd had from and with Colleen? Not that, either. You can't replace the love of your life, the center of

226 • Bill Pronzini

your universe. Maybe you could move on to someone else after a while, on a limited basis—and maybe you're just not made that way, no matter how much you hurt and how much you need. He wasn't, and it seemed Bryn Darby wasn't. Kindred spirits in that way, too.

So now he fully understood why he'd come here. Looking for something unattainable; looking for humiliation to purge himself of the idea. But he didn't feel humiliated; even the momentary shame was gone. All he felt now, limping through the cold night to his car, was empty—as if the hole inside him had been scooped out even wider.

That night, Colleen came to him in a dream. She walked into the bedroom and leaned over the bed. When he opened his eyes and saw her, he made a joyful sound and reached out for her. She stepped back, avoiding his embrace. "Don't do this," she said.

She was vivid to him in every detail; her whole body shimmered and glowed as if she were encased in a kind of haloed bubble. He sat up and reached for her again, whispering her name. And again she backed away.

"Don't do this," she said.

"I won't," he said. "No one else. Just you."

"Please don't do this."

"You're the only woman I'll ever love."

"No more," she said, "no more."

"I don't need anybody but you."

"Don't keep doing this to yourself, Jake. Promise me—please!"

He said, "I don't know if I can," and as soon as the

words were out the shimmery glow began to fade, she began to fade until he couldn't see her clearly any longer. He jumped out of the dream bed, his arms clutching emptiness. By then she was gone.

He woke up shaking. All the bedclothes were on the floor and the room was like a cavern of ice. He got the blankets up and over him and lay there afraid to close his eyes again, because when he did he knew he would see her in the same soft, fading focus as before.

"I don't need anybody but you," he said aloud. "I don't need anybody."

Lies.

Don't keep doing this to yourself, Jake. No more, no more.

21

JAKE RUNYON

In the morning he had himself under control again. Emotions in check, his professionalism hard-wired back into place. The fever of last night, the past week, had burned itself out; the disturbing sense that he might be cracking up was gone. There wouldn't be any more episodes, he'd see to that. He'd keep on functioning as he had been for nearly two years now, doing the job he'd been trained to do, existing in the moment. There was no other way. Opening himself up the way he had last night was like opening a vein and watching himself bleed to death.

The order of business today was the Youngblood pro bono case. He hadn't been paying enough attention to it. Focus on it, get it wrapped up, move on to the next. Youngblood's mother, sitting alone in that empty house of hers after her work, worrying, waiting for word—he owed her a quick resolution.

On the way up Nineteenth Avenue and through the park, he thought about what Bill had told him yesterday. Youngblood's ten-thousand-dollar borrow from Nick Kinsella, and the eighty-five hundred he'd laid on Kinsella three days ago to cover two-thirds of what he owed. Where'd it come from? Not from another loan shark; Bill was right about that. A friend? None of Youngblood's friends seemed to have that kind of money lying around. His mother? Same thing. Brandy?

Find out more about Brandy. He should've done that by now. Drag it out of Youngblood, if he couldn't get the information anywhere else.

First things first: Verna Washington.

The Lake Street apartment building where she lived was old San Francisco—cornices, bay windows, ornate stucco facade painted a pale salmon color. Three stories, four apartments each on the first two floors, two big flats on the top floor. Verna Washington lived in one of the apartments, second floor rear. When he rang the bell this time, he got an intercom response.

She was willing to talk to him. Buzzed him in, looked at his license through the peephole in her door, took the chain off, and let him inside. The apartment was cluttered, the furniture a weird mixture of old wood, fifties tubular chrome, and sixties bean-bag. One wall was painted black; the others were different shades of blue. Posters hung everywhere, most of them the restaurant-and-food variety, a few music-related. Rap music played, not too loudly, from an iPod on a glass-topped table. He tuned it out.

She stood with her hands on her hips, looking him over, smiling a little. Dré Janssen had called her "funky"; it was as good a word as any. She was small and round-faced, her hair done in uneven cornrows and colored an off-red, a small gold ring looped through one nostril, rings on all her fingers, and jangly bracelets on both wrists. Some kind of patterned caftan-type garment, African probably, covered her body from her neck to her bare feet. Her toenails were painted a violent purple. If she ever walked out of the kitchen at Bon Chance looking like she did now, there'd probably be a riot.

"Brian's in some trouble," he told her. "Could be big trouble. That's why I'm here."

"What kind of trouble?"

"I'm trying to find out."

"Well, you won't find out much from me. I haven't seen or talked to the man in more than two years."

"In touch with any of his friends?"

"Nope. Only met a couple and we don't hang in the same places."

"You know a woman named Brandy?"

"Who? Brandy?"

"The name's not familiar?"

"Never heard of her."

Nobody seemed to have heard of her. Mystery woman.

His capsule description of Brandy made Verna Washington laugh. "Putting me on, right? Brian with a sister looks and acts like that?"

"Not his type?"

"No way. I can't even picture it."

"How was he when you dated him? Seem to have everything together financially, personally?"

"Oh yeah, pretty much. Real serious about everything. And real religious."

"Nothing out of the ordinary about him or his life?"

"Nope," she said, and then grinned and said, "Not on the surface."

"How do you mean?"

"What you see ain't always all there is."

"I don't understand."

"Everybody got quirks. Underneath, you know?" she said. The grin again, and a laugh as if at some private joke.

"Look, Ms. Washington . . ."

"Verna. Never did like my last name, guess why."

Runyon ignored that. "What kind of quirk does Brian have?"

"Uh-uh. Personal stuff. Doesn't have anything to do with whatever trouble he's in."

"Why don't you let me be the judge of that?"

"Uh-uh," she said again.

He let it go. "Other people I've talked to say he's changed drastically in the past year or so. Started keeping to himself, spending large amounts of money, borrowing heavily to pay off debts, that kind of thing. Any idea what could've caused the change?"

"No clue. Brian I knew was Mr. Yup."

"Or where he might've gotten a large sum of money?"

"How large?"

"Several thousand dollars."

"Whoa. Not from anybody I know, that's for sure."

"I understand you and he weren't together very long."

"Not very. Just a casual thing, you know? He was never my boo."

"Boo?"

"Boyfriend. We only did the nasty once." She smiled again at the memory of it, a wry smile this time. "Brian wasn't a bed animal, you know what I'm saying?"

"Is that why you stopped seeing each other?"

"One reason. Total opposites, you know? We connected at Bon Chance, that's the restaurant where I work. Good-looking dude, real polite, bucks in his pocket . . . different from anybody else I'd been with. But the differences . . . too strong, man. No way we could've stayed hooked up."

A few more questions bought him nothing useful. He tried once more to get her to talk about this "quirk" of Youngblood's, but she stonewalled him again. Whatever it was seemed to amuse her.

What you see ain't always all there is.

Underneath, you know?

Cryptic phrases meaning what?

Brian Youngblood's address: no response.

Aaron Myers's address: no response.

He didn't like that. Something wrong in all this elusiveness; if he'd been tracking normally, he'd've sensed it before now. He rang the other doorbells in Myers's building, talked to two of the other tenants—one through the intercom, one in person. Neither of them had seen Myers in the past few days. Neither of them knew him very well. What kind of neighbor was he? Quiet, friendly enough but kept pretty much to himself. Brian Youngblood? Didn't know him, never heard the name before.

In the car, Runyon called Tamara on his cell. She didn't have much on Aaron Myers; from all indications he was a model citizen. What she did have was the name and address of his only relative in the Bay Area, a sister living in Pacifica.

Pacifica was a few miles south of the city, spread along the coast and up across the western hillside below Skyline Boulevard. It was part of the fog belt that stretched south from Ocean Beach in the city to Half Moon Bay; if there was fog anywhere in the Bay Area, Pacifica was sure to be socked in. There was fog today, thick and roiling, blowing inland on a strong sea wind. By the time Runyon came to the bottom of the long, curving section of Highway 1, the mist was so wet he had to use the windshield wipers.

Toward the middle of town, he turned down into a newish development of middle-class tract homes between the highway and the ocean. The Pacifica map he'd looked at before leaving the city indicated that the street Shari Lucas lived on was one of those nearest the highway, and he had no trouble finding it. Her house was like all the others on the block—nondescript, sea-weathered, its only distinction a front yard full of yellow and pink iceplant. There was an older-model Mitsubishi station wagon parked in the driveway.

Single mother, Tamara had told him, lived alone with her

two pre-school children, worked off and on for a firm of architects in the city. Child support from her ex-husband paid most of the bills. Like her brother, she seemed to be a model citizen.

He went up and rang the bell. The fog here was numbing cold, like vapor off dry ice, and heavy with the smell of salt. He stood hunched, hands in the pockets of his suit coat, until the door opened.

She was attractive in a thin-boned way, her hair clipped short, her eyes big and liquidy brown. She said, politely enough but with an edge, "If you're selling something, you can turn right around and walk away. I'm not interested."

"I'm not a salesman." He showed her his ID. "I'm here about your brother Aaron."

Her manner changed instantly. "Oh Lord," she said, "is he all right?"

"As far as I know."

"Has he . . . done something?"

"I'm not investigating him," Runyon said. "Could we talk inside? Pretty cold out here."

She let him into a living room cluttered with children's toys. Kid voices, interspersed with shrieks of laughter, rose and fell from another room at the rear. She said automatically, "I'm sorry, it's a mess in here." Then, "If you're not investigating Aaron, then who . . . ?"

"A friend of his, Brian Youngblood. Do you know him?"

"Met the man, but I don't really know him. He seems like a nice person . . . What kind of trouble is he in?"

"I can't answer that, Mrs. Lucas."

"But you think Aaron knows?"

"Yes. Have you seen or talked to your brother in the past few days?"

"No. Aaron and I . . . we're not close. He has his life and I have mine. I haven't seen him in months. But he—"

One of the kids let out a scream. She said, "Now what? Excuse me," and hurried out of the room. Runyon took a short turn around it, but there was nothing in there for him.

She was back inside of three minutes. "Kids," she said, but with a motherly affection. Then she said, "Aaron called me last night."

"Oh? Any particular reason?"

"I don't know, I wasn't here. Nobody was here. The kids were with a neighbor and I was out with a friend and I had my cell phone on voice mail. He left a message."

"Did you call him back?"

"Not last night. I . . . didn't get home until very late. I tried this morning, but he didn't answer at his apartment and he wasn't at work and his cell was off."

"What did his message say?"

"Just that he needed to talk to me. He sounded . . . funny."

"Funny?"

"Not like himself. Upset or worried . . . shook up."

"Is the message still on your voice mail?"

". . . Should be. I don't think I erased it. You want to hear it?"

"If you wouldn't mind."

She went and got her cell phone and played the message. It was a good quality unit; the voice and the inflections were clear.

"Sis, this is Aaron. I know it's been a while but . . . I need to talk to you. I really need to talk. If you're listening, pick up." A few seconds of humming silence. "Oh God. I don't think I can stand any more of this without . . . Look, call me back as soon as you get this, okay? It's really important."

"He does sound funny, doesn't he?" Shari Lucas said.

Runyon said thinly, "Yes, he does."

"He's involved in Brian's trouble. That's it, isn't it?"

"I don't know," he lied. "But I'll find out. Do you have a key to his apartment?"

She blinked at him. "A key? Why would you want—"

"Please, Mrs. Lucas. Do you have a key?"

"No. I never had need for one . . . Oh, sweet Jesus, you don't think something's happened to him?"

He pasted on a reassuring smile, pressed one of his business cards into her hand. "Do something for me, okay? Call Aaron's friends, see if you can locate him. And call me right away if you do. Will you do that?"

"All right, but . . . Can't you give me some idea of what this is all about?"

No, he couldn't. What he'd just begun to realize about her brother and Brian Youngblood had shaken him a little; it would knock her down. He said he'd call her later, or Aaron would, and got out of there as fast as he could without scaring her any more than she already was.

22

The damn cell phone started in again as I was driving to work Friday morning. I was on the curvy part of Upper Market and I had to wait for a break in traffic in order to pull over into curb space.

I barked a hello, and a woman's voice said, "This is Deanne Goldman. Mitch Krochek's friend?" She made the last a question, the way some people do when talking to strangers.

"Yes, Ms. Goldman."

"Mitch had to leave this morning before seven—an emergency at one of his job sites—and he didn't want to bother you so early. So he asked me to call and let you know he won't be available all day."

"When will he be available?"

"He didn't know. Probably not until sometime this evening."

"Ask him to call me when he gets in," I said. While she was saying she would, I had a thought. "Would it be possible for you to meet with me today? For a few minutes on your lunch hour, say?"

". . . Why?"

"A few questions I'd like to ask you."

"About what? I don't know anything about Mitch's wife."

"I'm sure you don't. Just some general questions."

"Well . . . I suppose it'd be all right."

"Suggest a time and a place that would be convenient."

It took her a few seconds. "There's Heinold's at the foot of Webster Street. Do you know it?"

"I've been there, yes."

"I'll try to be at one of the outside tables."

"What time?"

"Noon?"

"Fine," I said. "How will I know you?"

She described herself. I told her what to expect in return.

When I got to the agency I filled Tamara in on what had gone down with Phil Partain. "So now we've got the beating cleared up, but I can't see Partain as the person responsible for the disappearance. Two separate events."

"Who, then? Lassiter's out, QCL's out, Partain's out. One of her gambling friends? Somebody else she owed money to?"

"Possibilities, both. There's another, too: Mitchell Krochek."

"You think?" she said. "Why would he call you if he's responsible?"

"Smoke screen. Make himself look innocent if the law steps in."

"That'd mean he killed her and did something with the body."

"If he did kill her," I said, "chances are it was an accident—end product of a fight. He's not the premeditated type."

"Not the violent type, either, according to his BG."

"You don't have to be the violent type to lose control in a screaming argument. His wife gave him plenty of provocation and he's been on the ragged edge. Still . . . What's his first wife's name again?"

"Let me check the file." I went into her office with her while she brought it up on her computer. "Right—Mary Ellen Layne."

"What have you got on her?"

"Let's see. Not too much—I didn't go very deep. Remarried, one daughter. Lives in San Bruno, works here in the city—"

"Where?"

"Tarbell Jewelers, on Post."

Ten minutes from South Park. I said, "I think I'll pay her a visit, see if she feels like talking about her ex-husband."

Tarbell Jewelers opened at ten o'clock. The address was half a block off Union Square, which meant street parking was impossible; I left my car in the Square's underground garage and walked over to Post through a thin, misty overcast. It was five past ten when I got there. The two employees, one male, one female, gave me those bright-and-hopeful, early-morning looks that disappear when they find out you're not the first customer of the day after all.

The woman was Mary Ellen Layne. Krochek's age, conservatively dressed as befitted the surroundings—Tarbell's was one of the more exclusive downtown jewelry stores—and a general body double for Janice Krochek. Mitch evidently liked his women slender, brunette, high-cheekboned, small-breasted. Her professional smile evaporated when I showed her the photocopy of my license and asked if she'd mind answering a few questions about her ex.

"Why?" She said it softly, with a glance across at where the male employee was polishing the glass top of a display counter. He didn't seem to be paying any attention. "Are you investigating Mitch for some reason?"

"Not specifically, no. He's involved in a case I'm working on." Little white lie to maintain confidentiality and forestall a lot of questions and explanations.

The shape of her mouth turned wry and bitter. She leaned forward and said even more softly, "It has to do with a woman, I'll bet."

"As a matter of fact, yes."

"And not his wife. If he's still married to number two."

"He is."

"Amazing. She must be a saint."

"Why do you say that?"

"To put up with him this long. I divorced him after ten months, and I was a fool not to have done it sooner."

"He was unfaithful to you?"

"Oh, yes." No hesitation, no reticence about discussing personal matters with a stranger. I had the feeling the pump in her was always primed and ready when the subject of Mitchell Krochek came up. "Twice that I know about.

Twice in ten months. The first time . . . well, let's just say the honeymoon didn't last very long. If I'd found out about it at the time, I'd have left him then and there."

"He was pretty young then," I said. "Young men make mistakes that they don't always repeat as they grow older."

"Are you telling me he's turned into a faithful husband? I don't believe it."

"Once a cheat, always a cheat?"

"That's right. Mitch . . . well, it isn't just a roving eye with him. It's compulsive. He'll never be satisfied with just one woman. He needs a steady stream of conquests to boost his ego."

"And he doesn't really care about any of them, is that it?"

"Well, that's not exactly true. Give the devil his due. He cares for a while, genuinely, I think, but he just can't sustain his feelings. He—"

"Mrs. Layne." That came from the male across the room. "Do you need any assistance?"

"No, thank you, Mr. Tarbell." She reached down into the display case, brought up a bracelet bristling with diamonds, set it on the glass in front of me. "Pretend you're interested in buying this," she whispered to me.

I picked it up, gingerly. A discreet little price tag hung from one clasp. $2,500. Some bracelet. Kerry would love it. She would also give me a swift kick in the hinder if I bought her a piece of jewelry anywhere near that expensive.

"How did Mitch react when you told him you were divorcing him?"

"React?" she said. "I'm not sure I know what you mean?"

"Was he angry, upset over the financial implications?"

"No. He was just starting out at Five States Engineering and we didn't have much to divide between us, much less get upset about."

"Was he ever violent?"

"Mitch? Violent? Good Lord, no."

"Never raised a hand to you?"

"Never. I'll say this for the man—he was always a gentleman, in and out of bed."

"How would he handle a major argument?"

"The same way he handled everything else. Yell a little, whine a little, rationalize everything, and never accept responsibility. The two affairs that broke us up . . . it was the women's fault, they wouldn't leave him alone, *they* seduced *him*."

All of which pretty much coincided with my take on the man. I still had the diamond bracelet in my hand; it felt cold and hot at the same time and I put it down as gingerly as I'd picked it up. "How long has it been since you've seen him?"

"Oh, a long time. More than seven years. I ran into him at a party about a year after the divorce. We didn't have much to say to each other."

"No contact since then?"

"None."

"Do you know his second wife?"

"No. When I heard he got married again, I thought about calling her up and sharing some things with her. But I'm not really the vindictive type. And I expected she'd find out for herself soon enough what he's like." She leaned forward again, her eyes avid. "Has she, finally?"

I said, "I think they both know each other pretty well after eight years together," which I thought was a noncommittal response, but the words made her smile anyway. Mary Ellen Layne may not have been a vindictive person, and nine years is a long time, but she was still carrying a grudge. Not that I blamed her, if what she'd told me was an accurate portrait of her ex-husband.

Heinold's First and Last Chance Saloon was the oldest little piece of Jack London Square, a historical anachronism surrounded by the concrete, asphalt, and modern buildings that now dominated the Oakland waterfront. It was a literal shack built around 1880 from remnants of an old whaling ship, first used as a bunk house for men who worked the East Bay oyster beds, then converted into a saloon. It'd been in continuous operation ever since, with food service added when the Square began to flourish decades ago. Jack London himself was rumored to have hung out there with his pals in the oyster pirating game.

Deanne Goldman was seated at one of the umbrella-shaded outdoor tables when I arrived. There weren't many of them, so she must have been there a while; the place was already teeming with lunch trade. She was shorter and darker than Krochek's two wives, but cut from the same body mold and bearing a vague resemblance to Mary Ellen Layne. She wore a neutral expression that didn't change when I introduced myself and sat down, but there was nervousness behind it: she kept rotating a glass of iced tea in front of her without drinking any of it. A determined set to her jaw told me I was not going to get anything out of her about her boyfriend that she didn't want to give voluntarily.

The first thing she said to me was, "Have you found out anything yet about Mitch's wife?"

"Not yet."

"He's half-frantic with worry, poor man. He's so afraid that Janice is dead and he'll be blamed for it."

"If he's innocent, he has nothing to worry about."

"*If* he's innocent? Of course he's innocent." Her eyes narrowed; the determined jaw poked out a little farther. "He's your client, for God's sake. Surely you don't think . . ."

"I don't think anything, Ms. Goldman. I've exhausted a lot of possibilities in Mrs. Krochek's disappearance and there aren't many others left. I need to get as complete a picture of the situation as possible—that's why I'm here. He's told you everything about the situation, I take it?"

"Everything, yes. We don't have any secrets from each other."

"How long have you known him?"

"Eleven weeks. I know it's not very long, but that doesn't matter. You don't have to know somebody for a long time to love and understand them."

Wrong, lady. Some people you do; some people you could know for a lifetime and never understand. But I said, "When did he tell you he was married?"

"At the beginning of our relationship. That's one of the things I love about Mitch—he's honest, forthright, he doesn't try to hide anything."

"It doesn't bother you?"

"That he's married? Why should it? He doesn't love her anymore, and she doesn't love him. He loves me."

"But you know he doesn't want a divorce."

"Of course he doesn't. She's already squandered so much of his assets, why should he give her half of everything he has left?"

"He wouldn't have to give her anything if she were dead."

"He doesn't want her dead. He's not like that."

"Solve all his financial problems. And he'd be free to marry you."

"We don't have to be married to be together," she said. "I'm not a conventional person. The kind of relationship we have right now, based on love and trust . . . it's enough for me."

No, it wasn't; I could see it in her eyes. I said, "He told me he was with you Tuesday night from seven until after eleven. True?"

"Yes. At my apartment."

"He never left, even for a few minutes?"

"Not for one second."

"Did you see him on Wednesday?"

"No. You told him to stay home all day, and he did."

"I spoke to his first wife this morning," I said. "He tell you about her?"

"Yes. She's a bitch."

"Do you know her?"

"I'm glad I don't. I'll bet she had all sorts of nasty things to say about Mitch."

"Not really."

She rotated the iced tea glass again. "Why did you talk to her anyway? What could she possibly know about Janice's disappearance?"

"Nothing. As I told you, I'm trying to get a complete picture."

"By asking all these questions about Mitch?"

"Among other things. You think he'd object?"

". . . No, I guess not. He . . . has faith in you. He told me that."

"I hope I can repay it," I said.

"I hope so, too. You . . . well, you just don't know how bad it is for him right now. I probably shouldn't tell you this, but . . . he cried in my arms last night. Like a hurt child."

I didn't say anything.

"I felt so awful for him," she said. "He's such a warm, caring, loving man."

And she was a naïve young woman riding for a big fall. But it wasn't up to me to burst her rose-colored bubble; she would have fought me if I'd tried.

A waitress came by. I asked for the same as Deanne Goldman was drinking. The waitress asked if we wanted to order lunch and I said not yet and she went away. Ms. Goldman sat making more wet circles with her glass.

"It's not his fault, you know," she said.

"What isn't?"

"The affairs he's had. She told you about the one that broke them up, didn't she? His first wife?"

"She mentioned it."

"She drove him to it. Nagging at him all the time, denying

him . . . you know, in bed. He wouldn't have been unfaithful to her if she'd been a proper wife."

"Is that what he told you?"

"It's the truth," she said. Sharply, but with a defensive undertone. She had her own doubts, I realized then, even if she wasn't admitting them. If she were lucky, she'd burst the rose-colored bubble herself before Krochek had a chance to hurt her too badly. "He wouldn't have been unfaithful to Janice, either, if it weren't for her gambling sickness."

"With you, you mean?"

"With me, with that neighbor of his. He was vulnerable, he's still vulnerable . . ."

"Wait a second," I said. "He had an affair with one of his neighbors?"

"Before he met me. It didn't last very long. She wanted it to, but it was just . . . physical for Mitch. Not like it is with us."

"Which neighbor? Did he tell you her name?"

"The woman who lives next door to him. It was right after her divorce."

"Rebecca Weaver?"

"Yes," she said. "Rebecca Weaver."

23

JAKE RUNYON

Aaron Myers's car was a ten-year-old Buick LeSabre. He got that info from Tamara on the way back to the city. When he reached Noe Valley, he drove around within a three-block radius of Myers's apartment building. If he found the LeSabre, and Myers still wasn't answering his bell, he'd figure some way to get inside the building and then the apartment.

He didn't find it.

And nobody answered the bell.

Maybe good, maybe not. Depended on where Myers had gone. Runyon drove up to Duncan Street—and the LeSabre was parked around the corner from Youngblood's flat, facing downhill at a bad angle. There was a narrow space behind it; he squeezed the Ford in there and went to have a look. All the doors were locked, the interior empty. Under the windshield wipers was a parking ticket, issued at

9:40 that morning. A sign just down the way said that Friday was street-cleaning day and there was no parking on this side between four a.m. and noon. The Buick had been here since early morning or sometime the night before.

He didn't like that at all.

He hurried uphill and around the corner. He expected to have some trouble getting into Youngblood's building, but he caught a break. One of the residents had bought a new refrigerator; a delivery truck was double-parked in front, and two burly guys were hauling the old one out through the propped-open front doors. Runyon waited for them to pass by, stepped through as if he belonged there, and hurried up the stairs.

A one-minute lean on the bell bought him nothing but muted noise from inside. When he tried the knob, it turned under his hand and the door edged inward. The muscles in his gut and across his shoulders pulled tight. Cop's instincts, telling him something was wrong here—bad wrong. He stepped inside, shut the door softly behind him.

The place smelled of death.

The odor was so faint and indistinct that most people wouldn't have noticed. He'd been in too many places where people had died; the smell was sometimes strong, sometimes not, but always there and always the same.

He went down the hallway into the living room. And that was where he found Aaron Myers, slumped down in a chair in front of one of the computers, his head lolling sideways, his eyes squeezed shut.

Runyon touched knuckles against one cheek, felt the neck artery. Cold skin, no pulse. Dead a long time; rigor had already come and gone. Last night sometime. There were no marks on the body, nothing except a thin foamy drool that had leaked from one corner of the mouth and dried there. Overdose of some kind—hard drugs or prescription pills.

The computer in front of the corpse was turned on. Sleep mode, looked like. He wiggled the mouse with the back of his hand, and the screen lit up. Writing, more than a page single-spaced. Suicide note—he read enough of it to tell that. The rest could wait.

He backed away, his lips flattened in against his teeth, and turned to look around the room. No signs of disturbance anywhere in here. The way the flat was laid out, there'd be a bedroom at the front and another at the rear beyond the kitchen. The one in front, adjacent to the living room, would be the larger of the two. He checked in there first.

Drapes drawn, a lamp burning on a nightstand. And another dead man, sprawled backward across the bed.

No need to check this one's pulse. One side of his head had been caved in by a heavy blunt object—the brass lamp, a twin to the one on the nightstand, that lay streaked with dried gore on the carpet.

When you'd been on enough homicide scenes, you learned not to let the blood and torn flesh and staring eyes and cold waxy faces bother you too much. This was just another in a long string. Standard murder-suicide, the kind that happened almost daily in a city the size of San Francisco.

Except that it wasn't. Not this one.

The dead man on the bed was wearing black net stockings

and a blue silk dress. The dress had twisted open in front, exposing a pair of foam-rubber falsies; hiked up far enough on the thighs to reveal lacy, black silk panties. Close-cropped black hair showed where the hennaed wig had come undone. The face under the pancake makeup and crimson lipstick was lean, ascetic, the chin slightly beard-stubbled.

Brian Youngblood.

And Brandy.

One body, but for months now it had contained two personas—the quiet hacker and the foulmouthed bimbo. Half him and half her, even now in death. There was a walk-in closet across the room; from where Runyon stood he could see racks of women's clothing inside, four or five times as many garments as there were of men's wear. Brandy had been the dominant personality for some time.

There was no surprise in any of this. He'd begun to catch on as soon as he heard the voice-mail message on Shari Lucas's cell phone—the same voice that had said, "If you want to know who hurt Brian Youngblood and why, ask Nick Kinsella" in the anonymous phone call. Which meant Aaron Myers had pretended to be Brian Young-blood at Monday's interview. And Brandy, the mystery woman that nobody seemed to know? A couple of other sound bytes from his memory file had helped give him the answer. Ginny Lawson saying: "He's mentally ill . . . Sick, sick, sick." Verna Washington laughing slyly as she said, "What you see ain't always all there is . . . Underneath, you know?"

He should have figured it sooner, much sooner. Plenty

of clues, hints. The weird behavioral changes, Dré Janssen's comments. The normal way Myers walked on that first visit, while Brandy grimaced with pain when she moved in her chair—that alone should have tipped him to the switch. Youngblood was the one who'd suffered the recent beating by Kinsella's enforcer, Youngblood who'd still been stiff and sore.

If he hadn't been so focused on himself and Bryn Darby, he could've prevented this, saved two lives—

No.

None of this was his fault. You can't hold yourself responsible for the actions of others—that was a hard and fast truth you learned when you first went into police work. If you didn't learn it, you either quit and got into some other line of work or you stayed on and made a lousy cop.

Runyon turned away, went back out to where the other body slumped in the chair. Without touching anything, except the computer keyboard with the back of one knuckle, he read the rambling suicide note Aaron Myers had typed there.

I killed Brian. Only he wasn't Brian anymore, she'd taken over. Brandy. She kept hurting me. People been hurting me all my life but nobody as badly as her. She was a control freak, a monster. She made my life a living hell. I couldn't take it anymore. She deserved to die.

I didn't know Brian was like that, half man and half woman, until three months ago. He kept it a secret from everyone until Brandy began to take over. She'd been with him since he was fifteen, he said, making him wear women's underwear, dress up in women's clothes when he was by himself. Getting stronger and stronger every year until he was buying her expensive presents, clothes and jewelry and computers, spending more and more time with her, borrowing money from a loan shark so he could pay off his debts so he could buy her more presents. She didn't want him to marry Ginny, she was jealous of Ginny, so she told Ginny all about Brian and her and what they did together in bed.

Then she told me. She needed me to know. Not because I was Brian's friend, because she needed my help. Brian couldn't make me do what she wanted, but she could. Not then but later. I came over one day and there she was, all dressed up in those ugly woman's clothes, talking the way she did, calling Brian's mother names he never would have in a million years. She was jealous of Mrs. Youngblood too, she hated that poor woman. I don't know why. She'd never tell me. She was crazy.

It made me sick. But I couldn't get away from her. I tried to but I couldn't. I was afraid of her from the first. She had this way about her, a kind of power you couldn't resist. She could make you do things you never thought you were capable of. Not sex stuff, thank God, it wasn't like that, I don't know what I'd have done if she'd tried to, if she....

But what she did was worse, she made me steal money, embezzle money from the company I work for. She said she should have told me about Brandy sooner, made me steal the money sooner so Brian wouldn't have had to go to a loan shark. Today she wanted me to steal MORE money. Another five thousand to pay off the rest of what Brian owed Nick Kinsella. I couldn't do it again. I couldn't. I refused and she hit me, she said she'd kill me if I didn't do what she said.

She was out of control, a control freak out of control. If I didn't stop her she'd keep hounding me and hitting me and threatening me. I knew someday when she got mad enough or crazy enough, she'd do just what she said she would, she'd kill me.

So I killed her first. In self-defense. There wasn't anything else I could do. She deserved to die. I'm not sorry I destroyed the bitch.

But I'm sorry Brian is dead. He was my best friend and I killed him too. I can't live with that and I won't go to jail because of what I did to her. I'm a coward a miserable fucking coward I don't care what

That was all. Ended in mid-run-on sentence on the second page.

Runyon backed away again. All of it was clear now. That first day he'd come here . . . Brian in Brandy's persona, Myers pretending to be Brian at her insistence—find out what he wanted, why Rose Youngblood had hired a detective. Myers, weak, ineffectual, chafing under Brandy's lash but unable to break loose, making the anonymous call out of desperation. And when that didn't bring results quickly enough, when Brandy made her demand that he steal another five thousand from his company and threatened to kill him if he didn't, Myers swinging that brass lamp in sudden blind fury.

He returned to the bedroom, stood looking down at what was left of Brian Youngblood. He could almost see the headline in tomorrow's *Chronicle*: BIZARRE TRANSVESTITE MURDER-SUICIDE. Yeah, the media would love this. Even in San Francisco, where bizarre happenings were part of the norm, it was just kinky enough to warrant a big play—the kind that provokes smarmy comments and sick jokes.

Brian doesn't have anyone else who cares as much as I do. I'll pray for him.

It'd tear his mother up. Her only child, all she'd had in a life barren other than her religion. His death, even the money troubles and the collusion in Myers's embezzlement—with the help of her pastor, she'd learn to live with that. But the rest of it . . .

He kept staring at the body lying there in the ice-blue dress and the black net stockings. Lipstick, eyeshadow—you could scrub that off. The bloody dress and the stockings and woman's underwear and wig could be disposed of easily enough. Not so all those clothes in the closet, bottles of makeup on the dresser—but he could've been living with a woman, it could look that way in the preliminary stages.

Only one person besides him knew the truth about Brian Youngblood now, and Ginny Lawson wasn't talking to anyone about Brandy. Might come out later that Brian had been a cross-dresser, but by then it wouldn't have any media appeal. It was what he was wearing when he died, and the dual-personality angle, and Myers's suicide note that made it sleazy media fodder. One click of the delete button would erase the suicide note. With men's clothing on the body instead of the dress and underwear, with some of the details left out or glossed over . . .

Tampering with evidence.

Thirteen years as a police officer, another seven as a private investigator, and this was the first time he'd ever for one second thought of crossing the line.

Did it make any real difference to the law if the details of a conclusive murder-suicide were altered slightly? No. Would it make a difference to a bereaved mother and her memories of her son? Definitely. Strong arguments in favor.

But not strong enough.

He wasn't going to do it. Wasn't capable of doing it, for Rose Youngblood, for Aaron Myers's sister and her two kids in Pacifica, for anyone. Not because he might get caught, but because it would destroy one of the last things he had left that mattered to him: his self-respect.

He opened his cell phone and tapped out 911.

24

On the way into the Oakland Hills I tried to find a possible fit for Rebecca Weaver in the Krochek disappearance. Hard to do without more facts and the answers to a bunch of questions. And there might not be a fit. An affair six months old was a pretty cold dish to go digging around in.

Unless Mitchell Krochek had started sleeping with her again, or had been sleeping with her the entire time he'd been bedding Deanne Goldman. From what I'd learned about him, he was the type of man capable of maintaining two concurrent affairs, particularly when one of the women lived right next door.

Krochek had told me he'd talked to his neighbors after the disappearance, but he hadn't been specific about which ones. One of them must have been Weaver, given her proximity, and there was no reason for her not to have been candid with him if she'd seen anything out of the ordinary. Ms. Goldman had no idea one way or the other; he hadn't mentioned the woman's name recently. How did Weaver and

Janice Krochek get along? She didn't know, she said, but if there'd been any problems Mitch would have told her, he told her *everything* about his private life. Sure he did. She also claimed not to know anything about Weaver other than what she'd confided to me about the brief affair.

I'd've preferred to talk to Krochek before I interviewed Rebecca Weaver, but when I called his cell all I got was voice mail, and his secretary at Five States Engineering told me he was on a job site and incommunicado for the day. So I'd just have to wing it with Ms. Weaver—assuming she was home and willing to talk to me.

When I drove into Fox Canyon Circle, the three houses grouped around the cul-de-sac had an external look of desertion. No people, no cars, not even a sprinkler working in one of the front gardens. The whole area had a two-dimensional look under a high, fragmented overcast; the pale sun seemed caught in the gray-white like something in a web, its light silvery and shadowless. Despite a strong wind and the absence of humidity, it was the kind of day that makes me think of earthquakes. The sky had looked a lot like this when the Loma Prieta quake created several hundred square miles of havoc from Santa Cruz north to Sonoma County in '89.

I parked between the Krochek house and the one belonging to Rebecca Weaver. The wind bent and swayed limbs in the trees along the canyon rim, and you could hear it thrumming in the telephone wires. It was like a hand on my back as I walked up the front walk to the Weaver house.

When I pressed the doorbell, a few chords of some vaguely familiar song echoed inside. Cute. Like the song snatches that the cell phone companies used in place of a good old-fashioned ring.

Two minutes, and the door stayed shut.

I let the bell play its tune again. Same result.

Well, hell.

There was a flagstone path that wound through the fronting cactus garden. I went along there onto the Krocheks' property, following the route Rebecca Weaver had taken the day I'd met her. The front gate was closed but not locked. I went across the inner patio and pushed the bell there. Normal chimes, and as expected, no response.

It took me about fifteen seconds to decide to exercise a certain tacit right accorded me as Mitchell Krochek's representative. The Krocheks' spare key was still under the decorative urn at the front wall; I dug it out and used it on the door.

The coolness inside was faintly musty, the way houses get when they haven't been aired out in a while. All the drapes were closed tight, making it too dim to find my way around without turning on some lights. The telephone and answering machine were in an arched alcove off the formal living room. The blinking light on the machine indicated that there were two messages. The first was from one of the friends Krochek had contacted about his wife, asking if everything was okay; the second was a familiar male voice saying curtly, "Carl Lassiter, Mrs. Krochek. Call me." That one had come in at 2:45 yesterday afternoon, before my meeting with him.

I went into the kitchen. The dried blood smears were still there on the tile; Krochek had followed my advice on that score, at least. He hadn't touched anything else in there, either; the dirty dishes still jammed the sink, giving off the sour odor of decay.

Nothing had changed in the rest of the house, as far as I could tell. The empty Scotch bottle and overflowing ashtray and strewn clothing still cluttered the spare bedroom. The bed in there was unmade, the sheet pulled loose at the bottom corners—testimony to a couple of long, sleepless nights for Krochek before he moved in with Deanne Goldman.

Back to the kitchen and into the laundry room. A quick look around there told me nothing. I turned the deadbolt on the outside door and stepped into the backyard.

The narrow half-moon gouge in the lawn caught my eye again. I got down on one knee to look at it this time. Half-inch or so deep, which meant that it had been made by something heavy; the grass that hadn't been ground down into the dirt was brown and dead.

Wheelbarrow?

Could be. The width of the furrow was the right size for a barrow tire. And a wheelbarrow was a convenient way to move a body from one point to another. To a car, say, backed into the garage or up close to the garage door.

There was no sign of a wheelbarrow out here, but I thought I remembered seeing one among the other garden implements when I'd looked into the garage last time. I headed over that way. What stopped me before I'd taken a dozen steps was a smell carried on a gust of the cold wind. Rank, noxious—

Rotting meat.

The hair on my neck stood up like quills. When the wind

gusted again, bringing me another whiff, I followed the odor to a fenced-in section between the garage and the gate that led out front. Another gate opened into a narrow enclosure where the garbage cans were kept. Garbage smell, that was all. Except that it was too strong here, too distinct.

I eased the lid up on one of the cans. The stench that poured out was bad enough to make me recoil, start me breathing through my mouth. The can was stuffed with paper-wrapped packages and freezer bags, all of them showing bloodstains. At first glance I thought: God Almighty, he killed her and cut her up. But when I took a closer look, swallowing bile, I saw that it wasn't human remains the packages and bags contained, but steaks, chops, roasts, hamburger.

The second can was filled with more of the same. Plus brand-name bags of fruit, vegetables, fried potatoes; TV dinners and other kinds of quick meals. The sort of items you buy in the freezer sections of supermarkets.

Discarded and long-thawed frozen goods, all of it.

As if somebody had emptied out a freezer.

I slammed the lid down, backed out of the enclosure, and opened the side door to the garage. Dark, empty, the only odors those of oil and dust. I found a light switch and two rows of hanging fluorescents came on. The wheelbarrow sat against the near side wall, next to a propping of shovels, rakes, and brooms. Its metal interior was scored and dirt-streaked, but there were other, darker stains on the sides. I scratched a fingernail through one of them, held a fleck up for a closer look. Dried blood, all right.

At the far end was a loft supported by beams and heavy chains. Most of the storage space looked to be empty.

Below it, at the back wall, a plywood partition had been erected to create a small separate room. The sound of my steps on the concrete floor seemed loud and hollow as I walked back there, stepped through the doorless opening in the partition.

Storage boxes piled on one side, and on the other, set between the plywood and the back wall, a big floor-model freezer.

I knew what I was going to find even before I opened it. I took a couple of deep breaths before I lifted the lid. Through the icy vapor that wafted up I had a clear look at the dead woman inside.

She had been wedged in there at an awkward angle, knees drawn up, one arm twisted under her and the other down against her abdomen. Her eyes were open, staring; the coating of frost gave them and the death rictus of her mouth an even more repellent look. She wore jeans and a white blouse, the blouse splotched across the chest and stomach with frozen blood. The frost and the blood made it impossible for me to tell what had caused the wound or wounds that had killed her.

All of that was bad enough. But the biggest shock was her identity.

It wasn't Janice Krochek I was looking at.

It was Rebecca Weaver.

25

I lowered the freezer lid, quit the garage, and went back through the house and out the way I'd come in. Following a cold, prickly little hunch now. Nothing lost if it didn't pan out; another few minutes wouldn't make any difference to the law or Mitchell Krochek or the dead woman in the freezer.

I crossed the strip of lawn that separated the Krochek property from Rebecca Weaver's. All three of the homes here had the same general layout. The gate in the narrow fenced area next to the garage, where her garbage cans were kept, was unlocked. So was the second gate that gave access to her backyard. And so was the side door into the garage. I opened that one and looked inside. The car in there was a Pontiac Firebird, low-slung and sporty and either new or close to it.

All right. I went through the yard to the back door: also unlocked. Easy, so far. But if the rest of my hunch proved out, it would stop being easy pretty damn quick.

I eased the door open partway, leaned in to listen. Faint sounds somewhere inside, unidentifiable from here. I stepped through onto a utility porch similar to the Krocheks', then across the kitchen. The sounds were louder now—a familiar and discordant series of electronic beeps, clangs, and bongs. They stopped abruptly as I passed through the kitchen; I stopped, too. The new silence was heavy and unbroken.

The dining room, formal living room, and family room were empty. I made my way down a hallway that bisected the full width of the house, walking soft. Four doors opened off of it; the last one on the west side was open. I edged forward until I had a clear look inside.

It was like looking into some sort of surreal three-dimensional exhibit. Motionless shapes, shadows, one halo of stationary light, and one bright rectangle of shifting colored images in an otherwise darkened room. And all of it wrapped in a hush that put a strain on my eardrums, tweaked at nerve ends.

Spare bedroom turned into an in-home office—desk, chairs, couch, bookshelves, computer workstation. Blinds drawn, the only illumination coming from a halogen desk lamp and the computer screen. She sat hunched forward in front of the screen, her back to me and her body stiff with tension; the only part of her that moved, now and then, were the fingers of her right hand as they manipulated the mouse. The back of her neck and the ends of her hair were wet with sweat. A half-smoked Newport burned in a full ashtray on her left; ash littered the desk around it and the air was thick with smoke. An empty glass, a bottle of

Scotch, a woman's wallet, and a scatter of credit cards were on her right. I didn't need to see the silent monitor to know what was going on.

I went in there, still walking soft and at an angle until I was parallel with the desk and within the range of her vision. She didn't notice me; she was in a kind of trancelike zone, as if the images on the monitor had hypnotized her.

"Hello, Mrs. Krochek," I said.

I had to say the words again before they registered. Her head jerked sideways, but even when the brown eyes focused on me, there was no other physical reaction except a tightening of the muscles around her mouth. "Oh, it's you," she said with no discernible emotion. As if it was perfectly natural for me to be there. As if I were no more than a small, annoying interruption, like a buzzing fly.

The look of her was chilling. Hair wildly tangled, no makeup, skin sallow and moist, eyes bagged and feverish with excitement. Clothes wrinkled and soiled. Soiled body, too; the room stank of sweat and unwashed flesh mixed with the stale odors of booze and tobacco smoke. If she'd slept at all in the past three-plus days, it had been for no more than a few minutes at a time. If she'd eaten, it hadn't been enough to dirty more than the two plates and two cups that sat on the low table in front of the couch. Existing the whole time on Scotch and cigarettes and adrenaline.

Her eyes flicked away, drawn magnetically back to the screen. She stared at it for a few seconds, moved the mouse, moved it again. "Shit," she said then, still without any inflection. "Another loser. I should've kept on playing the twenty-line slots, let this damn site cool off a while longer."

She was playing seven-card stud now, I saw when I moved a little closer. She clicked on the ante for a new hand, or "posted the blind" as it's called, looked at her hole cards—king of diamonds, ten of clubs—and made a bet: $50. Reckless and foolish, without a pair in the hole.

"I had a hot streak going for a while," she said, "shooting the pickle and winning two out of three hands. At one time I was ahead fifteen thousand. Can you believe it? Fifteen thousand! I couldn't lose."

"But then you did."

"Yeah. My luck never holds for—Shit!" She'd lost another hand.

"How much are you down now?"

"I don't know. Twenty K, maybe. It doesn't matter."

"No? Why not?"

"Plenty more where that came from."

"Rebecca Weaver's money."

She didn't deny it; she was still in the fever zone. "I'll win it back," she said. "All of it. My luck's starting to change again. I can *feel* it."

"Credit cards? Or did you tap into her bank account, too?"

She didn't answer. Her eyes were fixed on the screen.

"Is that why you killed her? To get your hands on her money?"

". . . What?"

"I found her body," I said. "In the freezer in your garage."

Nothing until the hand being played was finished and she'd lost again. Then, as she posted the blind for a new one, "I didn't do it on purpose. It wasn't my fault."

"What happened?"

". . . What?"

"What happened with Rebecca, Mrs. Krochek?"

"She came over to my house. She said she wanted to see if I was all right but it wasn't me she was worried about, it was Mitch. She . . . Yeah, baby, that's it, that's it! Wired aces!"

The bet she made on the aces was $250. I didn't try to talk to her until the hand played out; she wouldn't have heard me. She lost that one, too—lost another $1200 of Rebecca Weaver's money on a single hand.

It was the amount of the loss that made me step forward and do what I should have done sooner: flip the switch on the workstation's power strip. She let out a yell when the screen and the desk lamp went dark. Sudden rage brought her up out of the chair, sent her flying at me with her hands hooked into claws and her nails digging at my eyes. I couldn't control her; in her fury she had a man's strength. The sharp nails got in under my guard and opened burning furrows down the left side of my face. I had no choice then but to clip her. It didn't hurt her much, but it knocked her down and drove the fight out of her. When I was sure that she wasn't going to come at me again, I hauled her up by the arms and pushed her down on the couch.

She said, dully now, "You son of a bitch."

There was a ceiling globe; I switched it on. In the stronger light, she made a pathetic, wasted figure slumped down on the cushions. The excitement had gone cold in her eyes. They were bleak, bloodshot, reflecting the light with the same empty glassiness of an animal's.

I pulled the chair out from the workstation, straddled it

in front of her. My cheek stung like the devil; when I touched the ragged furrows, my fingers came away bloody. I shook out my handkerchief, held it against the wounds. Sometimes it pays to be old-fashioned enough to carry a handkerchief.

"Why did you kill Rebecca Weaver?" I asked her.

"I didn't mean to." Her voice wasn't much louder now than a hoarse whisper. "She made me do it."

"How did she do that?"

"Real sweet at first, butter wouldn't melt in her mouth. But then she started ragging on me about hurting Mitch. I told her to shut up, go away, but she wouldn't. Just kept ragging, calling me names, bitch, gambling slut. You know what she told me then? Take a guess."

"That she had an affair with your husband six months ago."

"That's right. You know about that?"

"I know. But you didn't until she told you."

"Stupid. I should've known. Right next door, always looking at him like he was a piece of candy. *She* was the bitch, not me. Dirty little bitch."

"So you killed her."

"No, it wasn't like that. She . . . I was hung over, sick, and she kept ragging and ragging, saying how much better she was for him than me or that cunt he's sleeping with now. I told her she could have him, welcome to him, but that didn't stop her. Kept screaming at me, breaking my eardrums, and then she grabbed my arm and I . . . I don't know, I must've picked up a knife that was on the sink . . ." She shook herself, the way a dog does when it comes out of water. "I don't remember stabbing her. I don't. She was just . . . lying there on the floor, blood all over her, eyes wide open. Dead. She . . . I was sick, shaking so bad I couldn't think . . . I don't know, I don't *remember*."

"What did you do then?"

"Had a drink, a big one. Wouldn't you?"

I didn't say anything.

"I would've called nine-eleven if she hadn't been dead. I would have. I thought about doing it anyway. But the police . . . I couldn't face them. I was scared . . . real scared . . . You know what I mean?"

"Yeah," I said, "I know what you mean."

"I sat in the living room with another Scotch and tried to calm down. I don't know how long it took . . . a long time."

"And then?"

She licked chapped lips. "I need a cigarette. Give me one, will you?"

There was an open pack next to the computer. I got up to fetch it and a booklet of matches and the overstuffed ashtray. The smoke in there was bothering my chest, but I could stand it for the few minutes it would take to get the rest of the story out of her. Her hands trembled as she lit one of the cancer sticks; it bobbed between her lips, sending up smoke in erratic patterns around her head.

"All I could think about was getting her out of there. You know? No idea what I'd do with her, not then, but I wanted her out of my house. I . . . dragged her into the laundry room and out through the back door. The gardener, he'd left a wheelbarrow on the lawn. I wheeled it over and lifted her into it. Like a sack." She laughed, a sudden bleating sound that showed how close to the edge she was. "Like a big bloody dead sack."

"Then you wheeled her into the garage and put her into the freezer."

"No. I went back inside and washed the blood off the knife. I don't know why I did that. Blood all over the floor, but the knife, on the counter . . . I don't know why, I just did." She blew smoke in a ragged stream. "That's when I got the idea. While I was washing the blood off the knife."

"Moving in here, using her money to gamble with."

"She didn't need it anymore, did she? She was dead and I'm alive and I . . . why shouldn't I use it? Use her house, too, the goddamn bed where she fucked my husband."

I didn't say anything.

"She had her purse with her, she was going out somewhere after she finished ragging on me. I looked in her wallet. Credit cards . . . my God, she had a dozen! Big credit limits on every one, I checked later to make sure. So much money. Why shouldn't I spend it?"

"And that's when you put her into the freezer."

"I had to empty all the frozen stuff out first, so she'd fit. It wasn't easy getting her in there. A dead person weighs a lot."

Yeah. "How long did you plan on leaving her there? Until you gambled away all of her money?"

"I don't know. I didn't think about that. One day at a time, that's the way I've always lived. Thinking too much makes you crazy."

"Why didn't you clean up the kitchen before you came over here? The blood smears on the floor."

"Didn't I? Jesus, I must've been too distracted. And Mitch found them and called you. That's why you're here."

"I've been looking for you since Wednesday."

She waved that away. "Anyhow," she said, "I needed action real bad. The fever was eating me up. And I knew Rebecca had a computer . . . if she didn't have a password to log on, it'd be easy to use it. She didn't and it was."

"And you've been here ever since."

Jerky nod. Her cancer stick was almost down to the filter; she lit another one off the burning coal. "Except once when I ran out of cigarettes. I took her car, late, and went out and bought a couple of cartons and some more Scotch. Nobody in the neighborhood saw me. All alone here the rest of the time. Nice and quiet except when the phone rang or somebody rang the doorbell. My God, it was heaven! All that money, play as long as I wanted, shoot the pickle whenever I felt like it. I was ahead fifteen thousand at one point. Did I tell you that?"

"You told me."

"Fifteen thousand." The half-hysterical laugh again. "Top of the world, Ma."

"Only then you fell off."

"I'd've hit another winning streak if you hadn't showed up," she said. "I would have, I know it. Only a matter of time."

I didn't say anything.

She said, as if the thought had just come to her, "Does Mitch know?"

"Not yet."

"He'll be ecstatic when he finds out. No more worries for him."

"About you? Don't be so sure."

"He doesn't care about me," she said. "He never did. All he cares about is money and pussy." With sudden vehemence: "It isn't fair! He'll divorce me now and take everything and I'll get nothing."

I said, "That's not the way it works," and immediately wished I'd kept my mouth shut.

"It isn't? Why isn't it?"

Too late now. She'd find out soon enough anyway. "Committing a felony or a series of felonies doesn't invalidate the no-fault statute," I said. "It probably should but it doesn't."

She stared at me. A long ash fell off the end of the burning weed; she didn't seem to notice, didn't brush it off her lap.

"You mean I can still divorce *him* and get my half?" she said. "Half of everything—the house, the bank accounts?"

"You'll need it for a good lawyer."

"But not all of it." A slow, ghastly smile formed around the cigarette stub. "There'll be some left. Even if I have to go to prison, there'll be some left when I get out."

I lifted myself off the chair. The smoke in the room was making me sick. She was making me sick. Time, past time, to let the law have her.

"Maybe," I said, "but you won't keep it for long. Horses, slots, poker . . . not for long."

"That's what you think," she said. "I'm overdue for a real winning streak. I've got a big one coming to me, big and long. You wait and see. Top of the world and this time I won't fall off."

She believed it. Sitting there ravaged by her addiction, with another woman's blood on her hands, and chasing the high and beating the odds was all she cared about, all she believed in. In a way, that made Janice Krochek more unfathomable, more terrible to me than anything else she'd done.

26

Mitchell Krochek took the news hard. The main reason, of course, was that no matter what kind of legal strategies his lawyer indulged in, he would lose half of his assets in a divorce settlement. And be forced to make restitution for the debts his wife had run up on Rebecca Weaver's credit cards, and to shoulder responsibility for any civil claims that might be brought by her estate. As if that wasn't enough, he'd have to suffer the negative publicity the murder trial would bring. Yet I had the sense that under his selfish, rutting-male exterior, he genuinely cared for Janice Stanley Krochek—even now, after all she'd done and was about to do to him. Love's a funny thing. Sometimes, no matter how much two people beat the living hell out of it, it never quite dies.

It was late Friday evening that I talked to him. He called me at home, after the Oakland police finally contacted him. He seemed to need to talk. Kept thanking me for helping him, for "getting to the bottom of things"—saving his ass, he meant. Volunteered the information that he intended to put the house on the market right away because he "couldn't stand to live there now, after what she did to Becky in the kitchen. I'd have nightmares every goddamn night." He'd move in with Deanne, he said, until the house was sold and the trial was over and he could start living a normal life again. After that, well, maybe he'd marry Deanne. She loved him and she wasn't crazy like Janice and his first wife—"first woman I've ever been with who wasn't batshit in one way or another."

I liked Deanne Goldman and I wished her well, so I hoped he was right about her mental health. If so, she not only wouldn't marry him, she'd throw him out and change all the locks on her doors.

On Saturday morning, early, I called Tamara at home to fill her in on Friday's events. She had a few questions; when I'd answered them, she said, "Some Friday. For you and for Jake, too. Our first pro bono and it turned out crazy, blew up in a murder-suicide."

"The hell it did. What happened? He didn't get caught up in it, did he?"

"Found the bodies, that's all," she said, and provided details. "Weird, huh?"

"Very. Sometimes I think this agency is cursed. We get the damnedest cases."

"Always come out okay, though, don't we?"

"So far," I said. "One thing for sure after yesterday: I've had it up to here with gamblers and gambling. If there's even a hint of either one in a future inquiry, we turn the case down flat. In fact, do me a favor and don't even mention gambling to me anymore."

She let me hear one of her saucy little chuckles. "I won't," she said. "You can bet the house on it."

Sunday night, in bed, Kerry said, "I've made a decision."
"Good for you. About what?"

"The way I look."

"You look fine. Kind of sexy tonight, as a matter of fact. Is that a new nightie?"

"Don't try to change the subject."

"I didn't know I was. Since when is a compliment changing the subject?"

"I'm talking about cosmetic surgery," she said.

Uh-oh. "You're not serious?"

"Oh yes, I am. Very serious."

"My God, not one of those bizarre surgeries you and Tamara were talking about the other night . . ."

"No. Only my face."

"Nice face. I like it just as it is."

"You don't have to look at it in the mirror every day."

"I look at it every day straight on. Same thing."

"No. Not from my perspective. Lines, wrinkles, eyebags . . . on my best days I look my age. On my worst . . . bleah."

"Come on," I said, "you worry too much about things like that. Doesn't matter. You still think and act young, you're still sexy as all get-out—that's what's important."

"To you. Not necessarily to me."

"Vanity," I said.

"Call it what you want," she said with a little snap in her voice. Then, "What's wrong with a little vanity?"

"I didn't say there was anything wrong with it—"

"Men can be just as vain as women. More. It's human nature."

I sighed. "All right. So what is it you want to change?"

"Everything."

"A whole new face? Like Bogart in *Dark Passage*?"

"If I had my druthers," she said. "But I'll settle for a complete makeover. Get rid of the lines around my mouth, the eyebags and wrinkles. I've seen and talked to a few women who've had the procedure. They all look years younger. Just as important, they all *feel* years younger."

"Sometimes," I said carefully, "that kind of surgery doesn't work out the way it's supposed to. I mean, there can be complications. Some face-lifts don't heal right and the person ends up disfigured—"

"Oh, bosh. There's a tiny risk, yes, but there's a tiny risk in just about everything we do in our lives. Surgeons have all sorts of new methods that make the procedure perfectly safe."

"Famous last words."

"Will you please stop arguing with me?"

"I wasn't arguing, I was only—"

"I've made an appointment with a cosmetic surgeon," she said. "Dr. Hamadi. He's in the same building as my oncologist downtown."

". . . Appointment for when?"

"Next Thursday afternoon."

"You mean you're having it done that soon?"

"No. It's just a preliminary examination to make sure I'm healthy enough to go ahead with the procedure."

"Healthy enough? So even if this doctor says you are, there could still be complications . . ."

"You're acting like I'm going to apply for a heart transplant. It's a simple operation, done thousands of times every day with *no* complications whatsoever."

"We're not talking about thousands of women, we're talking about *you*."

Her mouth pursed. Stubborn, determined. "I'm doing this for me, not for you or anybody else. After all I've been through this past year, I think I'm entitled—whether you agree or not. A face-lift is safe, it's affordable, and I'm going to have it done and that's all there is to it."

I wilted a little. "How long is the recuperation?"

"Not long. A few days until the last of the bandages come off. I'll be housebound for a week or so, but I'll take some vacation days and then work from home. I'll be all healed in about six weeks."

"What about scars?" I said, thinking of the little tattoos on her chest to mark where the cancer radiation machine hookup had been applied.

"Tiny ones, hidden inside my hairline. You'll never even notice them once the incisions have healed."

"Yeah," I said.

"Stop looking so gloomy," she said. "When you see the new me, you'll wonder why you put up such a fuss." She leaned over to slide gentle fingers over the bandage that

284 • Bill Pronzini

covered my scratched cheek, then started chewing on my
ear. "Think of the benefits. It'll be like going to bed with a
younger, more attractive babe."

"I don't want an attractive babe, I want you."

That ended the ear-chewing. "Thanks a lot," she said.

"I didn't mean—"

"Good night," and she rolled over and turned off the
bedside light.

I lay there in the dark, for maybe the thousandth time
pondering the differences between men and women. The
only conclusion I reached was that in this particular case,
Kerry was right. The risk in a face-lift was minimal, and
she'd been through so much. If she had her heart set on it,
she was not only entitled to have it but entitled to my full
support. Okay, then. She'd have it.

Besides, as she'd pointed out, there were benefits for me,
too. Now that I considered it, a younger-looking, even sex-
ier Kerry was a pretty juicy prospect . . .

27

JAKE RUNYON

The call came in a few minutes before nine Monday night.

He was on the couch in the living room with the TV on for noise, watching a Spencer Tracy movie he'd never seen before. Long, busy day and he was tired, but not tired enough yet to sleep. His cell phone was the unit that rang, and it was in his jacket draped over the back of a chair. He muted the TV and got up to get it.

"Jake Runyon?" Tentative, a little anxious. "This is Bryn Darby."

It was a few seconds before he said, "Yes. Hello."

"I'm not calling too late?"

"No, it's still early for me."

"I almost didn't call at all. I wasn't sure . . ."

"I'm glad you did."

"Yes. Well."

"How did you get my cell number?"

"It wasn't difficult," she said. "I have a smart lawyer and you and the agency you work for have a very good reputation." Pause. "Tit for tat."

"How's that again?"

"You tracked me down, now I've tracked you down."

"What made you change your mind? About talking to me again."

"I'm . . . not sure. Your visit on Thursday . . . I kept thinking about it off and on all weekend." Pause, followed by an odd little chuckling sound—odd, he thought, because it had come out of only one side of her mouth. "Like song lyrics that get stuck in your mind."

"I understand."

"Do you? I suppose you do." Pause. "I was thinking . . . Maybe it would be all right if we . . . what you suggested on Thursday."

"Sat down over a meal or coffee and talked?"

"Yes."

"I'd like that," he said.

"There's a coffee shop on Taraval just off Twenty-third Avenue. The Royalty Cafe. Silly name, but the food's good—I go there for dinner sometimes. I'll probably do that tomorrow night."

"What time?"

"Six-thirty, seven."

"Either fits my schedule."

"Seven, then." Pause. "There's something you should know. I could wait to tell you, but this is as good a time as any."

"Yes?"

"My face . . . the entire left side is paralyzed. I had a stroke a year and a half ago and that was the end result. Facial nerve paralysis, it's called. The doctors say I may regain control of some or all of the muscles in time, but chances are I won't. Most likely they'll atrophy and the condition will worsen over time."

"I'm sorry," he said. "But if that happened, it wouldn't matter to me."

"It matters to my husband. That's why he divorced me."

"Then you're better off without him."

"It also matters to me."

He said it again: "But not to me."

"We'll see," she said. Then she said, "Good night, Mr. Runyon."

"Until tomorrow, Ms. Darby."

For a long time he sat motionless, his hands resting on his knees, staring at the muted picture on the screen without seeing it, focused inward.

Damaged goods. The phrase she'd used to describe herself the other night. Well, so was he damaged goods. That was the attraction, the central ingredient of his compulsion—that, and the loneliness. He understood that now.

He understood something else, too. About himself and Colleen and her fading image in his memory and his Thursday-night dream. What his subconscious had been trying to tell him was that it was time to let go of the past, time to stop mourning the dead. Colleen had been gone almost two years now. He would always love her, but loving and grieving were two separate emotions. He was still here, still able to function. But if he didn't start living again, she would fade completely away, and once that happened he'd be left with nothing, no hope. He'd be so deeply mired in emotional quicksand that he'd eventually be sucked under—a form of suicide as final as the real thing.

Don't keep doing this to yourself, Jake. Promise me—please!

"All right," he said aloud. "All right."